FREEDOM TRAIN

EVELYN COLEMAN

MARGARET K. McELDERRY BOOKS

NEW YORK   LONDON   TORONTO   SYDNEY   NEW DELHI

MARGARET K. McELDERRY BOOKS
An imprint of Simon & Schuster Children's Publishing Division
1230 Avenue of the Americas, New York, New York 10020

This book is a work of fiction. Any references to historical events, real people, or real locales are used fictitiously. Other names, characters, places, and incidents are products of the author's imagination, and any resemblance to actual events or locales or persons, living or dead, is entirely coincidental.

For information about special discounts for bulk purchases, please contact Simon & Schuster Special Sales at 1-866-506-1949 or business@simonandschuster.com.
The Simon & Schuster Speakers Bureau can bring authors to your live event. For more information or to book an event, contact the Simon & Schuster Speakers Bureau at 1-866-248-3049 or visit our website at www.simonspeakers.com.
Also available in a Margaret K. McElderry Books hardcover edition
Book design by Krista Vossen
The text for this book is set in Sabon.
Manufactured in the United States of America
1211 OFF
First Margaret K. McElderry Books paperback edition January 2012
2 4 6 8 10 9 7 5 3 1

The Library of Congress has cataloged the hardcover edition as follows:
Coleman, Evelyn, 1948–
Freedom Train / Evelyn Coleman.
p. cm.
Summary: Twelve-year-old Clyde Thomason's older brother is a guard on the Freedom Train, which is carrying the Bill of Rights and other documents throughout the country in 1948, but Clyde is also learning about rights and freedom as he is saved from a beating by an African American boy, and later returns the favor when men in their Atlanta suburb decide to show the "Nigras" their place.
ISBN 978-0-689-84716-5 (hc)
[1. Race relations—Fiction. 2. Freedom Train—Fiction. 3. Schools—Fiction. 4. Bullies—Fiction.
5. Family life—Georgia—Fiction. 6. Atlanta (Ga.)—Fiction.
7. Georgia—History—20th century—Fiction.] I. Title.
PZ7.C6746Fre 2008
[Fic]—dc22
2007000953
ISBN 978-1-4442-3652-7 (pbk)
ISBN 978-1-4442-3653-4 (eBook)

To those of us who recognize that the fight for equality of race and class and the fight against imperial power must be fought on the same battlefield. And to my grandchildren, Taylor Blayne Parker and Jody Santana Rhone— be brave, speak out! Never give up the fight for freedom, justice, and equality for all people.

Acknowledgments ★

First I must thank Anna Burgard and Janice Shay of Savannah College of Art's Design Press, for bringing this story to my attention. Without their support, encouragement, and Anna's fabulous editing I wouldn't have a story. And to Karen Wojtyla's wonderfully brilliant editorial direction, plus the encouragement of Sarah Payne, who forced me to get this manuscript ready—without whom, you would not have a book to hold in hand. And to the incredible copyeditor, Erica L. Stahler, thanks—good looking out.

Craig Harmon, director, Lincoln Highway National Museum & Archives; literally this book could not have been done without his assistance and his copies from the National Archives. Thanks, Craig, for all your support and guidance.

Thanks to Rutha Beamon, archive specialist at the National Archives.

The fantastic Marines themselves: John A. Brown, Theodore (Ted) Tintor, and Hank Steadman—I love you guys.

The "real" folk singer, Cabbagetown native and friend, Joyce Brookshire. And the other Cabbagetown gang, Leon Little, Mack Jones, and Patsy Wyatt Clontz (too young to remember, but willing to share her mom's stories).

The folks in the historical section of the Savannah Public Library.

My frogmen, without whom Chester and the second Chester

couldn't have lived: John B. Jensen, herpetologist, Georgia Department of Natural Resources; Walt W. Knapp, naturalist; Professor Tyrone Hayes, herpetologist; Gregory George, herpetologist, Atlanta Zoo; Michael Edwin Dorcas, Department of Biology, Davidson College, expert on barking tree frogs; and the folks of Allaboutfrogs.org/infor/species/barking.html.

The American Flyer guy, Richard White of Miami, Florida.

Larry Tye, author of *Rising from the Rails: Pullman Porters and the Making of the Black Middle Class*.

Train experts: Jim O'Hara, SHS Trains; Steven Blackburn; Sam Rapp; Jami Reid, editor, *Hot Box*.

Alexis Scott, publisher, *Atlanta Daily World*; and Portia Scott, great-granddaughter of publisher, *Atlanta Daily World*, who discussed the history of Atlanta with me and their relative Mary Ellis Odum. And, of course, the fabulous Charlotte Roy, former news manager, *Atlanta Daily World*, who graciously placed my article regarding firsthand accounts.

Charles H. Atkinson, avid Atlanta history buff; Dozier C. Cade, former news reporter for the *Atlanta Journal-Constitution*, who covered the Freedom Train; George Goodwin, former news reporter for the *Atlanta Journal-Constitution*. Joyce Burns and Doris Jackson of the Atlanta Public Library. And my friends at the African American Research Library: Francine Henderson, Janice Sykes, and Sharon Robinson.

★ CAPTAIN CHESTER SAVES THE DAY ★

Phillip Granger was the most ornery, hateful body that ever stepped foot in our school, and he never stopped proving it. He was in my class 'cause they kicked him out of his fancy private school. Seemed like we was getting the punishment, though, seeing as how he tortured us all. A couple days before Christmas vacation weren't no different. I was minding my own business when I heard, "Pst," from two rows back.

Miss Fowler clapped her hands and said, "Get out your history books and read silently, class."

"Pst. Pst. Pst."

I didn't look back. I opened my book. "Pst. Pst. Pst." The "pst's" was gettin' louder. I twisted in my seat and saw Phillip Granger smirking at me.

"Hey, Clyyyyde," Phillip whispered.

Phillip always said my name like it was as bad as eating a pile of dookie. His pa was a boss at the cotton mill. Phillip didn't waste any time throwing it up in our faces, that his pa told our mas and pas what to do. Ain't nothing we could say about it neither, since it was true. We just had to grin and bear it.

Phillip smiled and held up a torn Marvel comic cover. "Look'ee, look'ee."

"You better give it back to him, Phillip," Ronnie said. He sat in the middle row, between us. He was my best friend since we was little.

Phillip, half standing, reached across two people and gave him a pluck in the head. "You better stay out of this, that's what you better do, Ronnie Shumate."

"It's okay, Ronnie," I said. "My brother is gonna send me another just like that one." I didn't know that for sure, 'cause I hadn't had a chance to tell Joseph that Phillip Granger had snatched my comic and tore it. It was his latest attack in a long list of meanness, and I didn't want Joseph to think I couldn't stand up for myself.

Now I was about to explode. But I didn't want no more trouble. Just yesterday me and Phillip went at it in the field after he snatched the comic book out of my hand. It was the cover with Captain Marvel and the Freedom Train. I only had it 'cause my brother, Joseph, was one of the marines guarding the train. But like always, Miss Fowler only saw me doing the scuffling, and she give me the whupping instead of Phillip.

"Pst. Pssst."

I guess I needed to make my life more miserable. It wasn't enough that I was the shortest twelve-year-old in seventh grade. Or maybe it wasn't enough that my blond hair had a permanent cowlick that people teased me about. 'Cause I did what I shouldn't have done—looked back again, just asking for it.

Phillip held up the Captain Marvel cover. He balled it up slowly in his left hand. Then he hawked a glob on it.

I hunkered down as Phillip's bony fingers squeezed the paper tighter, the muscles in his arm flexing. I knew what was comin' next. I squinted my eyes at him like Ma does when she's warning me 'bout something.

Miss Fowler was rummaging around at her desk. I cleared my throat so she'd look up.

Phillip threw the spitball.

Miss Fowler didn't see nothing. Seemed like she weren't never looking when Phillip did something bad.

I ducked.

But not soon enough.

Splat. It hit me and popped off onto the floor beside my chair. I could feel the slime of Phillip Granger's spit on the side of my ear. I grabbed for the handkerchief in my shirt pocket. And that's when I knew I was doomed, 'cause Chester—that was my frog—started squirming.

I'd packed him in my pocket that morning with some moss, wet dirt, and grass underneath my handkerchief. He'd been so still and quiet I'd forgotten 'bout him. Now I poked his head back down. I said as quiet as I could, "Stay still."

Chester hated being poked. I felt him pushing to get out. I grabbed him. That got him riled, and he told me so, in his itty-bitty-dog barking tree frog voice.

Miss Fowler's head jerked up. "Who is making that noise?"

One of my favorite things about frogs and crickets is there ain't hardly no way to tell where the sound they're making is coming from. I tried to sit still, squeezing Chester's sides to keep him from hopping out. But he just yelped louder.

Miss Fowler stood up calmly, like nothing was going. Just watching her, you wouldn't guess she was 'bout to snatch up her ruler. It was twelve inches long, and mostly every kid knew how to measure on account of it. Six inches of it done hit me just yesterday, and my hand was still smarting from it.

Miss Fowler gave the evil eye to each one of us, like she could see right through to our brains and read our minds.

Slapping the ruler on her palm, Miss Fowler walked between the desks. Then she held up her hand so we could see how red it was, just to show us she meant business.

Each of us looked down hard at our book, aiming to look innocent.

Then Chester started squirming, trying to escape. I squeezed him harder, just for a second. He barked—*Quit it!*—real loud.

I had to think fast or I was a goner. I did a fake hiccup and hoped Miss Fowler would think that was the noise she heard.

Miss Fowler said, "All right, I've had quite enough. Who is making that noise? I know a real hiccup from a fake one, and that was most certainly a fake one."

I wondered, *How could anyone know the difference between a fake hiccup and a real one?*

Someone said, "Where can I learn how to do fake hiccups, Miss Fowler?"

Then the entire class started hiccuping and laughing.

Miss Fowler was boiling mad now. She smacked her hand again as she walked past me to the back of the opposite row and slammed her ruler down on a desk.

I don't know what come over me, 'cause most times I ain't no tattletale. Maybe it was 'cause I hadn't seen her so mad before. Or maybe, I s'pose, 'cause she was already walking back my way, but all of a sudden I blurted out, "Phillip Granger threw a spitball at me."

Miss Fowler appeared to get taller. "Phillip Granger, what has possessed you?" she said, and cracked him across his knuckles.

"Ow!" Phillip yelled.

I had to give it to Miss Fowler, when she got mad, she'd whack anybody.

"It wasn't me!" Phillip shouted.

"Are you yelling at me, Phillip Granger?" Miss Fowler said, her eyes stretched open, her finger pointing at Phillip, her face as red as her hair. "No one shouts at me in my own classroom, young man."

Chester pushed to get out. I squeezed again, he barked again. I couldn't keep squeezing him, or I'd kill him. I just dropped my head. Unless Miss Fowler believed Phillip was the best ventriloquist in all of Fulton County, it was all over for me.

Now Miss Fowler was really fired up. She spun around and peered over the rims of her black cat-eye glasses as she came toward me.

"See, right there," Phillip said, pointing at me, "by his desk. He just dropped the spitball he was gonna throw at me."

Miss Fowler leaned over and examined the balled-up paper with the end of her ruler. "Isn't this that Marvel comic book with the Freedom Train on it, Clyde Thomason?"

"I-I-I . . . I-I-I didn't do it. Phillip Gra-a-anger threw it at *me*."

"Clyde, you're the only student with one of these Freedom Train comic books. Are you letting someone else take the blame for your shenanigans? That's perfectly all right," Miss Fowler said, walking to her desk. She laid down the twelve-inch ruler and picked up Mr. Justice.

"But I-I-I . . ."

"Not another word," Miss Fowler said. "I don't want to hear it. Your brother is the pride of Cabbagetown, and you've destroyed the gift he sent you just to make a spitball. An ingrate, that's what you are, Clyde Thomason."

Weren't no call to say nothing now, stuttering or not.

In Miss Fowler's hand was a big old wood paddle in the shape of a flattened-out baseball bat that had MR. JUSTICE printed on it like a first grader done wrote it with a nail. Kids said Miss Fowler scratched the name on it with her fangs.

Miss Fowler pulled her chair in front of her desk and sat down facing the class. She patted her knees. "Come forward, Clyde Thomason, Mr. Justice is waiting."

I stood up and took a step toward her, but I couldn't really see her anymore. My eyes went all blurry. I reached for my handkerchief to wipe off some of the sweat. But when I pulled it out, Chester jumped out too.

Hop, hop, HOP. Oh, *no*!

Chester was a handsome frog. He was green, like summer leaves, with black spots dotting here and there. He was always smiling, and he had a purty yellow throat, a short, pointy head, and a full, fat, slimy body. But it seemed Miss Fowler didn't care 'bout the looks of no frog. She threw Mr. Justice onto the floor, jumped up screaming, "Heavens," and ran out of the room.

I grabbed for Chester, thinking I could say a big green bugger had popped out of my handkerchief. But 'bout that time Chester hopped over a boy and three girls. Most of the girls went to squealing and jumping up on their desks.

"Come on, Chester, quit playing around," I said. But before I could nab him, he hopped onto Phillip Granger's head.

Phillip looked like a bear had got ahold of him. The next thing I knew, he was hopping around crying, and I mean really crying, all snotty nosed. He ran around in a circle, with Chester clinging to his head like a rodeo cowboy on a steer. Chester wasn't 'bout to be knocked off. Who'da thought someone as nasty as Phillip Granger would be scared of a bitty old frog?

I kept snatching at Chester, but it's hard to catch a frog when somebody is hopping around with arms flying and they're taller than you. I finally jumped up onto a chair and grabbed Chester. I said to him, "Thanks, Chester, you saved me from a whupping—at least for a while."

But Phillip didn't give a hoot that I hadn't gotten a whupping. 'Cause he shouted at me from across the room, "You knew I hate frogs. That's why you brought him, ain't it? Well, I'm gonna get you for this, Clyde. I'm gonna get you good."

And I knew Phillip Granger meant it.

★ A VISIT TO ANOTHER WORLD ★

Before I could explain that I didn't have no notion 'bout his feelings for frogs, there was Miss Fowler at the door with the principal, Mr. Leon Little. I stuffed Chester back into my pocket just as Mr. Little motioned for me to follow them.

Mr. Little was new to the school and to Cabbagetown, but not Georgia. He was from Atlanta. Even though Cabbagetown was a part of Atlanta, they were 'bout as different as the sun from the moon.

Miss Fowler said, "Mr. Little, Clyde Thomason deserves a whipping for his disruptive and disrespectful behavior." Then she stormed off in the opposite direction.

Mr. Little looked right at me and said, "Come with me, son," in a very nice voice.

I dragged behind him a few steps, my stomach all knotted up. If only Mr. Little would disappear, then I could run on home. I was thinking what would happen if Mr. Little disappeared when I noticed his dark brown hair almost touched the back of his neck. No wonder some of the teachers said Mr. Little needed a good haircut. I'd also heard Mr. Little wasn't as mean as the teachers thought he oughtta be. I wasn't sure about that, but I figured even if he didn't whup me, my pa would whup me for getting in trouble to start with.

Mr. Little stopped and turned around. "Why are you walking behind me, son? Come on."

I walked next to him. The old principal, Mr. Sampson, didn't want students to get near him, and he sure wouldn'ta let them walk beside him. Mr. Sampson led and you followed.

Once we got to the door of his office, Mr. Little said, "Miss Fowler says she's so upset she has to visit the nurse to get her blood pressure taken. She wants me to tell your parents about this."

"P-p-please d-d-don't tell them, sir," I begged.

"I won't, this time," Mr. Little said. "But I hope you have learned why you shouldn't bring frogs to school?"

"I tried to keep him quiet, honest. I didn't mean for him to get out of my pocket. He's ornery like that sometimes."

"You're right, barking tree frogs can be ornery," Mr. Little said. "Since you're aware of that, you know better than to bring him to school."

"How'd you know Chester's a barking tree frog?" I asked, surprised.

"Miss Fowler said the frog sounded like a little dog. I'm somewhat of a herpetoculturist myself."

"A what?" I asked.

"A person who keeps and breeds amphibians or reptiles is called a herpetoculturist because they're part of a larger group called herps. 'Herp' comes from the Greek word *herpeton*, which means basically 'creepy, crawly things that move around on their bellies.'"

"Wow. I never knew that. So you're like a scientist, too?"

"No, the person who studies amphibians and reptiles is a herpetologist. People like us, we just like frogs and keep them around."

"Oh," I said, feeling a little less scared. I didn't know an adult other than Joseph who paid any mind to creepy, crawly things. Mr. Little had to be a nice man if he liked frogs. I said, "I just brung Chester to school today because he was feeling sorta lonely."

Mr. Little said, "'I just *brought* Chester to school.' Now, come on into my office, Clyde."

I sat down in the big wooden chair. The chair had wide, open slats in the back, kinda like jail bars. I figured that's the point. That's why you have to sit in it when you're in the principal's office for being in trouble—it's the school's notion of prison. I had lots of experience sitting in this chair when Mr. Sampson was principal. But this was my first time with Mr. Little.

"A lonely tree frog, huh," Mr. Little said. "I see. Son, how are you doing in your studies?"

I shrugged. "All right, I reckon." I didn't say nothin' to him 'bout me being lonely. That nobody paid attention to me no more. That Ma was always working. And Pa, since he got put to part-time work at the train, was moping around, and everybody kept on bragging on Joseph and saying nothin' good 'bout me, like I was invisible or something.

"You mean 'All right, I think.' Are you excited about the Freedom Train?"

I nodded.

"Why don't you tell me something about it? I understand your brother keeps you informed in his letters home. For instance, how many guards does the train have?"

I sighed. I'd answered these questions a million, zillion, gatrillion times. "There are twenty-seven guards. There's a hundred twenty-seven documents, including the Declaration of Independence. And . . . the train is taking them to more than three hundred cities in these forty-eight states. Joseph was chosen because he was a hero in World War Two. He saved the life of one m—"

"That's fine, son. I've heard good things about your brother. Now let's talk about you, and your reciting the Freedom Pledge when your brother and the train come to town."

I sat up.

About that time a teacher came to the door. "Mr. Little, sorry to interrupt you, but we need you," she said.

Mr. Little looked at her. "Can it wait?"

She shook her head.

Mr. Little said, "I'll be right back. Stay where you are, son."

While he was gone, I thought about what I'd got myself into. Why couldn't I just do it? No matter how bad I wanted to get up on that stage in Atlanta and recite them words, I just couldn't. I just couldn't.

Mr. Little and the other teachers had decided that since my brother, Joseph, had gone to the school, then fought in the war, and was now guarding the Freedom Train, it was only fitting for me to say the Freedom Pledge and receive the fifty-dollar prize from the mayor. I gotta admit, that prize looked real good to me. I could help Pa by paying for my American Flyer train with it. But every time I got up in front of people to speak, I got so scared I wanted to throw up on my shoes. After the second practice, I'd made my decision not to do it.

That's when Phillip Granger volunteered to say the Freedom Pledge. If it had been anybody else, I don't think I woulda minded. But thinking on him doing it just 'bout knocked me out. If I'd had a tail, it woulda been down between my hind legs.

Mr. Little came back into the office. He sat down. "I apologize for that, son. Let's get back to our talk. Miss Fowler tells me you have trouble speaking in front of the class—that you get nervous and stutter. Is that true?"

I nodded, but I didn't look him in the eye. All I could think was, *Miss Fowler's sure got a big ole fat mouth.*

"I also understand that because of this you've decided not to speak at the program for the Freedom Train. But don't you think you should try, since your brother was handpicked as one of the marines to guard the train?"

I mumbled, "I just can't do it, sir."

"Son, a lot of people right here in Cabbagetown would never get to see those documents if the train didn't stop here. I wouldn't want you to regret not speaking later in your life. And I'm sure your parents will be disappointed."

I wanted to tell Mr. Little that my folks didn't even know I was alive. All anybody cared about was how Joseph was making everybody so proud.

The bell sounded for school to let out. Mr. Little went on like he didn't hear it. I wondered if he was gonna whup me. I didn't see no strap where Mr. Sampson used to keep it, just a big empty nail on the wall behind the desk.

"Maybe you should reconsider, Clyde," Mr. Little said. "Some of the greatest speakers and singers have had problems with stage fright. That's what it sounds like you might have . . . but you can overcome that. It just takes a little practice."

Miss Fowler appeared at the door with her arms crossed, wearing the meanest look. "I hope you are going to whip this boy, Principal Little." Then her eyes got wide, and she backed up a few steps, pointing her finger and using her high, squeaky voice. "Why is that hideous creature still in this building?"

Chester had poked his head up. "He was just trying to get some air, ma'am," I said. I pushed the top of his head back down into my pocket.

Mr. Little said, "Well, Miss Fowler, we've settled it without corporal punishment, haven't we, Mr. Thomason?"

No adult had ever referred to me as Mr. Thomason. And I wasn't even sure what *corporal* punishment was, but I was glad Mr. Little thought we was settled up.

And what happened next wasn't nothing I coulda guessed.

Mr. Little stood up and shook my hand. "You're a fine young man, Clyde Thomason. And I think it's good that you understood your frog was lonely. The next time, though, just remember not to bring Chester to school."

Miss Fowler said, "What? Is that *it*? What on earth is his punishment?"

Mr. Little smiled. "He's already been punished, Miss Fowler." Then he looked at his watch. "School's out, son, go on home."

I had to squeeze past Miss Fowler. When I looked back, her mouth was flung open wide enough to catch a bushel of flies.

I'd never met a grown-up like Mr. Little before. I felt that instead of going to the principal's office, it was more like *Planet Comics* #7, "Weird Adventures on Other Worlds."

★ GETTING HOME — ALMOST ★

The minute I stepped out of the school door, I spotted Ronnie.

"What happened? You get a licking?" he asked.

"Nope," I said. "Mr. Little ain't so bad. Not like old man Sampson, that's for sure. He even done took down that big leather strap."

"I been waiting around for ya."

"Yeah. Thanks. Let's go," I said. I knew why he was waiting. He was scared Phillip and his boys would get after him, 'cause we were best buddies since first grade and all.

A black cat crossed the street in front of us. "Hold it," Ronnie said. He took seven steps backward, spun around, and spit on the ground.

"Whatcha do that for?" I asked, thinking I didn't really want to know.

"Black cat's bad luck. I gotta reverse it. You got any salt?"

"No," I said. "I don't think that's gonna help none."

"Suit yourself. It's okay, I got my lucky rabbit's foot in my left pocket. And it ain't just any lucky rabbit's foot neither. It's the *left* foot, and it was killed by a cross-eyed man using his *left* hand."

"I know, I know." I shrugged and shook my head. Ronnie was right proud of that rabbit's foot, and what did I know? Maybe it could work.

We walked to his front door. He lived on the far end of Reynoldstown, that's the next neighborhood over from Cabbagetown. His pa owned a store that sold all kinds of stuff. Sometimes kids made friends with Ronnie just to get candy or sneak peeks at the comic books. But he knew I wasn't one of 'em, since me and him been friends forever.

Besides, I wasn't much into store candy. My favorite was ice cream from the Hunkie cart. Just thinking 'bout that stick of vanilla ice cream covered with thick, hard chocolate made my mouth water.

"I still think you oughtta be in the celebration for

the Freedom Train," Ronnie said. "You speak good in front of me. Whoever recites the Freedom Pledge is getting fifty whole dollars from the mayor."

"I told you, I ain't gonna do it."

"Aw, go on, it'd make your ma and pa proud. You can talk in front of people when you try. I wish we'd entered the national Freedom Train essay contest like your brother said we should. We could've won in place of that girl from California. I would've wrote one called 'What the Marines Guarding the Freedom Train Do All Night Long.'"

"How was you gonna write that? You don't even know what they do."

"Sure I do, you read me Joseph's letters enough times. They sleep and guard, guard and sleep," Ronnie said, cackling like a hen. "You could've done it too. You could've wrote 'bout how the train is powered by a two-thousand-horsepower diesel locomotive named the Spirit of 1776. Shoot, that's like writing history down. On account of Joseph, you know more 'bout that train than any of us do."

"Only thing I can do is stutter and almost pass out in front of people," I said. "Remember the Sunday-school play?"

"So? You didn't hurt yourself none when you passed out. And the Salvation Army lady said that till you started sweating like it was raining, and stuttering and shaking like you was in a earthquake, you was doing all right."

"It don't matter. I ain't doing it."

"What about Joseph? You know he thinks you gonna be on that stage. Your ma said he's excited about you being up speaking and all."

"Yeah, well, I ain't never said I was gonna recite no Freedom Pledge. Besides, I don't care nothing 'bout no train, 'cept the American Flyer."

"You know that ain't so. You carry on about Joseph and that train every single day. Anyways, you think your folks gonna get your Flyer for you for Christmas? Let me see that ad again."

"I hope so," I said, pulling the American Flyer ad out of my pocket and handing it to Ronnie. "Be careful, I done looked at it so much it's coming apart."

"I'm gonna be careful," Ronnie said, looking at it.

"She's a beaut, ain't she? Pa's been saving up some money. He knows all I want is that train. I sure don't want no roller skates like I been getting every year."

"*Ronnieee*," Mrs. Shumate called. She had a *really*

loud voice for a tiny woman. She stood in the doorway, wiping her hands on her apron. "What you boys out here doing?"

"Gotta go," Ronnie said. "You gonna be okay getting home? I'll walk you real quick."

"Heck, I just walked you," I said. When we was younger, I'd walk him home, then he'd turn around and walk me home. Sometimes it went on for hours, till it got dark. Finally one of our folks would make us quit.

Mrs. Shumate said, "You ain't walking nowhere but in here to help me with the store." She walked back in the store singing a song real loud.

Ronnie said, "I guess I'll see ya tomorrow."

"*Ronnieee*, get in here *now*."

I nodded. Ronnie's ma could be crazy as a bedbug sometimes. No need to get her all riled up. "Yeah, tomorrow," I said.

He waved and walked inside the store.

I headed home. I slowed up when I got near the roundhouse. That's where the colored men worked for the railroad, repairing rails, fixing engines, wheels, and all kinds of stuff. Sometimes I could hear them shouting out to each other.

I heard somebody calling after me. I felt butterflies in my stomach. It was gettin' on dark. Chester was squirming again. I took him out of my shirt pocket and held him.

I saw three of 'em, on bikes. I knew who it was.

I was sweating so much it was hard to even hold Chester in my hands. It felt like somebody done poured a bucket of water on me.

"You better start running, Clyyyyde," Phillip Granger shouted.

Believe you me, I wanted to run something fierce, but I was froze to the spot.

Phillip threw his bike down—hard. I reckoned he didn't care if it got busted up, 'cause his pa would just get him a new one. He picked something up, but I couldn't make out what it was. He walked toward me, slowly.

"I'm gonna whup you to a pulp, chicken liver," Phillip shouted.

Beecher Stokes—we called him BB 'cause he used to walk around with a broken BB gun slung over his shoulder—wasn't saying nothing. Him and Jimmy Ray was Phillip's slaves. They did whatever he told 'em to. I couldn't make it out, how they come to be this way even though I'd known 'em all my life. They lived two streets over from me in the village. Until Phillip came, they never gave nobody no trouble. BB cheated playing steelies, and Jimmy Ray might lie on you, but that was 'bout as mean as they got before Phillip. Now they just followed him around like they's horses with bridles. They both laid their bikes down and walked over near Phillip.

"I-I . . . ain't wa-wa-wanting no . . . no . . . trouble Phi-Phi-Phillip," I said, feeling mad that I didn't just take off running. When Joseph come back from World War II, he told me he was done with fighting. He said a brave man knows how to stay out of a fight, not get in one.

BB said, "Come on, Phillip. Let's get outta here. Somebody might see us."

Phillip grinned; he was holding something behind his back. "We down here at the roundhouse, ain't nobody *to* see us."

I stuck Chester back in my shirt pocket and got in a fighting stance, like Joseph done taught me before he was in the war. Left fist up higher than right fist, fool my opponent. Make 'im think I was gonna do a uppercut with my left, like I was a lefty, which I wasn't, 'cause I was really gonna hit 'im with my right.

"There's men over there." BB pointed toward the roundhouse.

I could hear the sound of steel being hit with hammers. Loud shouts.

"Who? Them Negras? They ain't gonna mess with no white boys."

I was about to say he ought to listen to BB, when everything went black. I couldn't hear or see nothing no more. It was like I had finally disappeared—or died.

Then all at once I could hear almost like somebody whispering, "You crazy. Look what you done." It was BB.

"Let's get out of here," Jimmy Ray whispered. "Shoot. This ain't right. What you hit him with a plank for? We used to fighting fair and square in the village."

"Don't nobody care what you Cabbagetown hillbillies do," Phillip said. "Shut your traps or I'll give you both some of this!"

A shadow come over the top of me. I could barely make Phillip out. He held the plank up high. So that was what hit me. I could feel myself thinking, Well, it's over now.

Suddenly the shadow moved away. I could hear words louder now, somebody swearing.

"What the heck."

Ping. Bam. Ping.

"Stop it," Phillip yelled.

Ping. Bam. Bam. Ping. Bam. Ping. Ping.

"Ouch. Ouch. Ouch." I could hear Phillip, BB, and Jimmy Ray yelping like hit dogs.

Some light come back to my eyes. I heard them running away. Shouting, "Whoever you are, we gonna get you."

For one split second I saw a face. Then I blacked out again. The next thing I knew, I was on a porch settee with a wet towel over my face. I reached up and moved it. It was a man's face I ain't never seen before staring down at me.

"What's your name, son?" the colored man asked me.

"Cl-Clyde Thomason," I said.

"Where do you live, Clyde?"

I sat up, still a little woozy. "I live in the village, you know, Cabbagetown. Where am I?" I said. What was I doing with a colored man?

The man pushed me back, not hard. "My son

came and got me. It seems some boys jumped you. My son—come over here, son," the man said, waving. "My son ran them off. He's a champion with a slingshot. Got a three-wheely he made himself. But you were bleeding a little so I brought you here and patched you up."

"I had to help you out," his son said. "Three against one isn't fair." He held up his slingshot and smiled at me, proud like.

I ain't never seen a slingshot for three rocks at one time before. I bet Phillip was smarting about now. Served him right, too.

The boy said, "I'm twelve. How old are you?"

"I'm twelve," I said, touching my head. I could feel a bandage on it. It was throbbing. "Thanks for helping. But I gotta get home. It's late, and my ma and pa'll be looking for me."

"No problem, son," the colored man said. "I'll drive you home."

"No," I said, almost like I was shouting. "I'll walk myself home." I didn't know what Pa would do if I come home in a car with a colored man. I never even really talked to a colored person before. Ain't no colored people in the mill village.

"It's no bother, son. I'm Dr. William Dobbs Jr., and this is my son, William Dobbs the Third."

"Good to meet you. And I thank y'all, but I gotta get home," I said, sitting up. Things was swimming around in front of me.

"You might feel a little dizzy for a while," Dr. Dobbs said. "Son, I think you best let your doctor check you out tomorrow."

"My ma and pa ain't much for doctors. But I reckon I can go to the mill clinic. The cotton mill's got its own clinic and a place for you to get your teeth worked on. But I ain't been there before, not unless it was when I was real little," I said.

"Are you sure I can't take you home?" Dr. Dobbs said.

"I'm sure," I said. I gotta be honest—a part of me wanted him to drive me home. 'Cept a taxi once or twice, I ain't really been in no car. I stood up, kind of wobbly, like a newborn puppy. Now at least I could see better.

It was light over my head. I stared up. I ain't never seen a light on a porch in the ceiling before. It was even a fan up there. I could see inside the living room of the house. It was awful fancy. I said, "Where do y'all live?"

Dr. Dobbs smiled and put his arm around his son. "We live here. We moved here this month."

I didn't want to seem dumb, but I ain't know no coloreds lived in this part of Reynoldstown. I knew where we was. I could see that we was in the white part of Reynoldstown, where the biggest and best houses were. I almost asked, "Are you *sure* you live here?" but I didn't say nothing. I just tried to steady myself so I could go on home.

And that's when I saw it. Through the window. Inside on a table. I near 'bout passed out again.

Dr. Dobbs said, "What's the matter, son? You look like you've seen a ghost."

"Is—is—is that a . . . a . . ." I couldn't even get it out of my mouth. I was pointing.

His son said, "An American Flyer?"

I nodded.

"Yep. It's an old one, though. I'm receiving a new one for Christmas. Right, Dad?"

"Yes, Santa Claus thinks you've been a pretty good boy this year."

I said, "Me too, I'm getting one," but I wasn't even truly listening no more. I heard him, and a part of my brain wondered, if his son was my age, how come his pa was still talking about Santa Claus, but I didn't or couldn't say nothing. I just stood there, holding on to the chair back, staring into the living room at the American Flyer. He even had the entire set, with a whole town all around it, with little men, women, children, and even a dog.

"You want to come in and see it?" the Third William asked me.

That's how I'd started thinking 'bout him—as the Third William. I ain't never know no one personal that's counted their name as one, two, and three in one family.

"Come on," the Third William said. "I'll even let you play with it if you are up to it."

I ain't gonna lie. I wanted to go in there something bad and play with that train. I could've tasted it. But I couldn't bring myself to go in a colored person's house. Ain't nobody never told me not to, it ain't come up. But deep down I knew my pa wouldn't have liked it.

So I just said, "Naw, that's all right. I best be getting on home."

Dr. Dobbs helped me off the porch. "I'll walk you to the edge of Cabbagetown. How about that?"

I still wasn't sure I wasn't gonna fall over dead, so I said, "Okay." I felt my shirt to see if Chester was still there. But he was gone. I said, "Shoot."

"What's the matter?" Dr. Dobbs asked.

"I done lost my frog."

The Third William said, "I saw those boys take something from your pocket."

"That's where I had him. His name's Chester," I said, still patting my pocket.

"I'll look for it tomorrow," the Third William said. "Where do you go to school?"

"Grant Park," I said.

Dr. Dobbs said, "I'm friends with your principal there, Mr. Little. If William finds Chester, we'll give him to Mr. Little for safekeeping."

I didn't say nothin', but I know I musta looked like I'd swallowed a water moccasin. I ain't know there was white men friends with the coloreds. Not like *real* friends.

"Where you go to school at?" I said to the Third William.

"I attend David T. Howard."

"Oh," I said. I didn't say nothin' else, but I knew that was the colored school. That was dumb for me to ask.

"Bye," I said. I felt sick. Not only had I been hit in the head, but I'd lost Chester, too. What a stinking bad day.

Dr. Dobbs walked me across the railroad tracks to the edge of Cabbagetown. I could hear the mill, loud and clear.

"Good night, son. Take care," Dr. Dobbs said, and walked back toward Reynoldstown.

★ CABBAGETOWN ★

Now, I've walked that path home a million times, but it sure was different walking it after being whacked in the head and ending up on a colored family's porch. I thought about all kinds of things on the walk home. Seem like my head was full of scary thoughts. I jumped every time I heard the least little sound. Twice I thought I heard bicycles coming and hid behind a bush. It's times like these I miss Joseph the most.

I was proud he was on the Freedom Train, but I missed him something awful. Sometimes I felt funny when folk was bragging on him all the time. Ronnie said it was jealousy. I don't know about that, 'cause I did love my brother. I was trying not to blame him when nobody paid attention to me. After all, it weren't his fault. One thing was for sure, if he were home, Phillip Granger wouldn't have dared hit me with a plank.

We live just east of downtown Atlanta on the railroad line. Outsiders know where we live as Cabbagetown, but we just call it the mill village. That's 'cause the houses was all built by the Fulton Cotton Mill, which sits right dab in the middle of where our folks work. Just a few years back even the children worked there, until they changed the laws.

Our house is what's called a shotgun house. That's 'cause if you was to stand at the front door and shoot a shotgun, the bullet would go on out an open back door without passing through any walls.

The houses is all pretty much the same wood frame, peeling paint, two small windows, one on each side of the door, a tiny covered porch, and if you were lucky, a patch of grass instead of red mud and dust.

For winter the houses got a fireplace, where we burn coal. Come summer we all just bake up—it get so hot the air you breathing burns your nose.

The mill's founder, Jacob Elsas, built the houses in

the 1800s for the mill workers. People complain that the houses are too close to the train tracks, are too small, and shake like crazy when the train rolls through. But that's just Cabbagetown. We're used to it.

People say Cabbagetown got its name 'cause a man who was selling cabbages off the back of his truck turned it over and wrecked it, and then some of the folk around here come out and took his cabbages. Then others say it's 'cause people who had to work in the mills would put cabbage on to cook all day, while they's at work. I don't know which is true, but it ain't like it smells like cabbage, or everybody's got a bunch of cabbage patches around or nothing.

Rumor is a lot of the people here were sharecroppers. But I ain't never met no sharecroppers in Cabbagetown. My ma is from Cartersville, where she says they farmed "on the halves." That means they worked somebody's land, and they kept half of what they grew, and the person who owned the land got the other half. She says it wasn't never as fair as it seemed. My pa is from Barnesville, not too far away. But it don't matter none, though, 'cause wherever they come from, Cabbagetown folk don't much cotton to strangers.

It don't matter to me that we live close to the tracks. I love trains, wondering where they're going and what they carrying on 'em. My pa used to work as the switcher at the CSX railroad terminal right up the street, but since the war he works in Atlanta at the big train station. But only half-time now.

The only thing I do mind about where we live is the racket. The mill runs twenty-four hours a day making cotton bags for packing. There's loud rumbling and clanking in your head, day and night. Sometimes I feel like we live inside of a motor. The house shakes like somebody with the black lung disease. And since the mill done added a vat machine called a bleacher, it smells like puke two or three times a week. But it's home, and I reckon there's folk who have it worse.

I could see the kerosene lanterns were on in the house. Most of us in Cabbagetown ain't got no electricity or running water yet. Some did, though, and Ma wanted that more than anything.

I stood on the porch getting my breath before I went in. I figured they was eating supper by now.

"What happened to you, boy?" Ma said, jumping

up from the table when I walked in. She went right for the bandage on my head.

"Where you been all this time?" Pa asked, putting down his corn bread. "Who done this?"

I told 'em what happened—well, not everything. I don't rightly know why, but I couldn't tell them that the doctor and his son that helped me was colored folk.

Pa said, "I told you to leave that Granger boy alone. Good thing folk was there to help you. You hurt bad?"

I said, "No, sir. I was ready to fight, but he hit me with a plank."

"Rotten boy," Ma said quietly. "Go on and wash up for supper."

I sat down to a plate of black-eyed peas, collards, and fatback. I had two helpings of corn bread. Getting hit in the head was hard work.

"I'm gonna talk to old man Granger 'bout his boy," Pa said. "Ain't no call for him being such a devil."

"Leave it be," Ma said. "You know how Granger is. He don't want no women at the mill nohow. That might just give him cause to let me go."

I grabbed my glass and gulped some buttermilk.

With Pa working only part-time, I knew we needed the money that Ma brought home. But Pa didn't like her working.

"I done told you to quit. It was all right when the war was on and the women worked to help out, but now y'all need to be home to take care of the house and the young 'uns."

"I don't want to hear no such talk. What young 'uns? Ain't nobody here but Clyde, and he's near half grown," Ma said.

I didn't want to hear them fussing, so I asked Pa if I could go get some coal from out back. I come back in quiet like, stoked the fireplace, and cleaned off some of the soot, then went to my room.

That was the good thing about Joseph being gone—I finally had my own room. Well, just me and Chester. But now Chester was gone too. I felt sick. When I was getting ready for bed, I'd do the same thing every night. First I'd put Chester down for bed. He slept in a glass gallon jar that had moss and stuff for him. The jar used to have pickles in it. Ronnie Shumate give it to me from his pa's store. If I didn't put Chester in the jar, he hopped around all night. Barking tree frogs are the night owls of frogs.

Then I'd take out my American Flyer ad, straighten it best I could, and pin it to the wall. But tonight I didn't have Chester to put down, so I just pinned my ad up.

I hoped Chester found some place wet and damp just like he liked it. I hoped Phillip didn't hurt him like he hurt me. Joseph says some folk think frogs ain't no good as pets 'cause they don't have feelings like dogs and cats. But Joseph says they don't really know. I bet Chester missed Joseph. I sure did.

I lay out on the bed and looked up at the map Joseph sent me. I had colored pins stuck in it for where he had been so far. Since I ain't never been outside of Atlanta, I couldn't even imagine some of the things Joseph wrote me about.

He sent me a picture of this Golden Gate Bridge in a place called San Francisco and a picture of a China town, and it weren't even in China. I couldn't really understand how that could've been, but Joseph said he saw it with his own eyes, and he ain't one for lying.

Joseph's always been the smart one. After the war he got made sergeant at Camp Lejeune in North Carolina. Then one day he said a dispatch come in for corporals and sergeants to volunteer for a special duty. They wanted marines who was five feet eleven inches in height to six feet one inch. On the day it was time to pick, about 225 men showed up. An officer told them it was too many, so he went on through and picked twenty-five of 'em. Then it was narrowed down to eight and Joseph was one of 'em. I could almost hear him talking when I read his letters. He sure had learned how to write good.

First they went to Cameron Station in Alexandria, Virginia, for training. That's when they found out what their real mission was—to guard the Freedom Train with all its important documents.

During the training they was taught all kinds of stuff, including how to use the right knife and fork. Turns out they get invited to lots of fancy places to eat on account of them guarding the train.

I pulled my journal out. Nobody even knows I have a journal except Joseph. He's the one who give it to me. At first when Joseph told me he kept a journal, I laughed at him. "You mean like a girl?"

"No. Girls keep diaries," Joseph said. "Men keep journals. I'm going to be a writer one day."

"A writer?" I said. "What does a writer do?"

"He writes."

"That don't seem like a job."

Joseph laughed. He said that writers watch what's going on in the world, then they write about it. He said writers can change the world. Make folk think about something that's been there all along but they ain't paid no attention to it. He asked me, "Who do you think writes the newspaper?"

I ain't never even thought about it. All I knew was Ma said God wrote the Bible, and that was all we had to read in our house, besides my schoolbooks.

The first time Joseph come home from the war, he give me the journal. He told me how if he hadn't been able to write out stuff while he was fighting, he would've gone mad. He said war weren't what he was expecting, up close. And he swore he didn't never want me fighting. He said rich people get the poor people to die for 'em since "time memorial," whatever time that is. Then he give me this journal and said, "Whenever you thinking about something, write it down."

I write late at night. 'Bout half the words is spelled wrong. But lately I been trying to do better 'bout that. I wrote a little bit about all the stuff that happened today. But then I heard Ma coming, so I shoved my journal under my pillow.

"You all right, boy?" Ma said, coming into the room. "You better get to sleep before school tomorrow." She sat down on my bed. She touched my bandage. "You best stay away from that spoiled Phillip Granger."

"I'll try, Ma," I said.

"You say your prayers?"

"Not yet."

"Well, say a prayer for your brother. Where all he been so far again?" Ma said, looking at my map. On my wall with my map was my Flyer ad, Li'l Abner and Joe Palooka comic strips about the Freedom Train, and a picture of Joseph and the other guards in their dress blues.

Under my pillow was the picture of that movie star, Lana Turner, getting on the Freedom Train that Joseph sent me from a newspaper. It wasn't on the wall 'cause I didn't think Ma would want her pinned up there.

Almost every night Ma wants to hear where Joseph's been to. I know it by heart now without even looking at the map. "He started in Philadelphia, Pennsylvania, then he's been to New Jersey, New York, Connecticut, Rhode Island—"

Ma said, "Rhode Island, did you say? I just ain't never even heard of that place."

Ma says that every night when I get to Rhode Island. The first time she asked me if it was a island that was just a road. I told her, "No, ma'am, it ain't spelled like 'road.'" Ma and Pa only went to the third grade in schooling, so I have to do the reading and writing for 'em.

"I sure got a lot to learn," Ma said. "I'm so proud of your brother. He done been all over our country learning. Go on, now," Ma said. "Where else?"

"Massachusetts, Vermont, New Hampshire, Maine, Delaware, Maryland, District of Columbia, Virginia, North Carolina, South Carolina, and Florida."

Ma stood up. "Just think, our own Joseph being in all them places on that map." Ma shook her head. She rubbed my hair down. "You got your pa's wavy hair," she said, smiling. "Good night, baby."

Sometimes I hate if Ma calls me "baby," but tonight I didn't much mind. I said good night back and turned over. I said a prayer for Joseph, Ma, Pa, and Ronnie. Then I added on Chester.

I was tuckered out. Next thing I knew, I was fallin' off to sleep. I thought about the Dobbses. I sure hoped Phillip never found out it was a colored boy who rocked 'em. If he did it would be too bad for the Third William—and even worse for me. My last thought was that maybe Ronnie was right, maybe I did need a rabbit's foot, a left foot that's done been killed by a left-handed, left-eyed man. I sure was gonna need something to protect me now that the Third William done hit Phillip Granger with them rocks on my account.

⋆ WHOO! WHOO! ⋆

I tried to remember what Ma said about staying away from Phillip Granger. So when I got to school, I just went straight into the classroom.

Ronnie said, "Man, what happened to your head?"

"I'll tell you later," I said.

Phillip Granger strolled into the room, all tough and smirking. He looked straight at me and acted like he was swinging a bat.

I acted like I didn't even see him. 'Course I did.

Miss Fowler looked up from grading papers. She saw my bandaged head. "Clyde, what on earth happened to you?" she said, sounding real concerned.

She wasn't good at holding a grudge, even if she was mean as a snake sometimes.

"I fell," I said.

"Into a plank," Phillip said under his breath.

I didn't even turn around. I didn't want him to see my face turning red.

"Well, you let me know if you need to go see the school nurse," Miss Fowler said. "Class, this is our last day before the Christmas break. The next time I'll see you is on January first when the Freedom Train arrives in Atlanta. So let's practice and make sure we get this right. We want to make our school and town and parents proud, don't we? Margo, you start."

Margo stood up. She had long blond hair and eyes as blue as the sky. Every boy in the room sat up and stared at her, including me. I don't fancy girls much, but for some reason I liked looking at her.

Margo cleared her throat. "We are here today in Atlanta, Georgia, to celebrate the Freedom Train on this day, January first and tomorrow, on January second, 1948. The Freedom Train was organized by the attorney general of the United States and endorsed by President Harry Truman. All good citizens want to see the Freedom Train."

Miss Fowler nodded. "Now, Phillip, tell us what the Freedom Train stands for."

Phillip stood up. He marched close to my chair and bumped me with his knee. He leaned over and said, "I'm gonna get you and whoever rocked me. Just you wait."

I looked at Miss Fowler to see if she'd seen him bump me or at least stop to talk to me. But she was talking to Margo.

Phillip stood up front now, holding his paper. "The Freedom Train is a chance for all Americans to reflect on why they sacrificed during the Depression and World War Two. President Truman believes it is time for a rededication to the principles that founded our country."

I could feel anger boiling in me like a kettle on the stove. Why did Miss Fowler give him all the good parts? It wasn't fair. Joyce Brookshire had said she wanted to have something important to say, but instead Miss Fowler assigned her to be one of the documents. But Joyce refused, and now she ain't even in it at all.

Margo continued, "No other nation has ever sent its most precious treasures and documents of freedom out for the people to view."

Phillip spoke again: "The Freedom Train has seven cars. A baggage car, three Pullmans, where the staff sleep, and three exhibit cars."

It weren't right that Phillip got to tell 'bout the train. I should've been the one telling it. It was my brother that was guarding it. 'Course, it was my own stupid fault that now my only job was to help keep the documents straight when they got in line.

"Very good! Very good," Miss Fowler said. "You can go back to your seat, Phillip. Now, where are the documents?"

This was the goofy part. Kids were dressed to look like the documents on the train. It looked pretty stupid to wear two pieces of cardboard tied over your shoulders on strings. I was glad I didn't have to be a document. That was just plain embarrassing.

But Miss Fowler loved them documents. She just smiled and smiled at 'em all.

"I am the Declaration of Independence," Sally Wentworth began.

Phillip snickered in the back row. I turned around to give him the evil eye.

At first I thought he was laughing at Sally. But then I saw his bony hand go up.

Phillip always had some nasty suggestion to add to the documents' performance so's to make 'em feel bad. Like maybe they should wear something on their heads. Or maybe the documents should stand up straighter, more proud. He picked on the kids playing the documents near 'bout every day.

Miss Fowler held her palm up for the next document to wait a minute. "Yes, Phillip?"

Phillip put a serious look on his face, like whatever he was about to say was as important as any document on the train. "I was just thinking the documents could add a little 'Whoo! Whoo!' at the end, like the train's whistle."

Two documents' jaws dropped open. The Bill of Rights whispered, "Oh, no."

"Why, Phillip, that is a brilliant idea," Miss Fowler said. "Thank you. Now, documents, please . . ."

I wanted to shout out, "That's just plain stupid, and Phillip Granger knows it. He just wants to see the kids act dumb." But I didn't say a word. I just stared into space, wishing that Phillip Granger didn't exist. There weren't no doubt in my mind that Phillip would pick on the documents and "Whoo! Whoo!" them to death for the rest of the year.

Miss Fowler said, "Let's continue, and this time, documents, add a little 'Whoo! Whoo!' at the end. Yes, I like that. It makes it more exciting."

No one said a thing.

"Billy White," Miss Fowler said, "go on. I believe it's your turn next."

Billy was the tallest boy, and he always wore overalls that were so short they looked like he was expecting a flood. He walked up front, his cardboard flapping against his knees. He looked about as happy as a bear with his foot in a trap.

"I am the Magna Carta," Billy White muttered, pulling on his overalls. He gulped twice, his giant Adam's apple bobbing up and down. "Whoo! Whoo!" he said, and quickly moved over for the next document.

Miss Fowler said, "One more time, Billy. This time louder, and speak more clearly. And for heaven's sake, put some excitement into your 'Whoo! Whoo!'"

Billy repeated, "I am the Magna Carta. Whoo! Whoo!" with about as much excitement as a snail on a log.

Miss Fowler said, "Keep practicing when you get home."

The next document marched up front. "I am the Bill of Rights. Whoo! Whoo!"

I could hear Phillip snickering. He was having a grand old time.

"I am the Gettysburg Address. Whoo! Whoo!"

"I am the U.S. Constitution. Whoo! Whoo!"

"I am . . ."

I stopped listening to the documents. There were 127 documents aboard the Freedom Train. But sure as shooting, fifteen people pretending to be them was too many. And now with them adding the "Whoo! Whoo!" it was even dumber and more annoying.

Our school had been handpicked by the mayor of Atlanta to be a part of the celebration. We would be up there on the train platform with Mayor William B. Hartsfield himself.

Miss Fowler reminded us every day that we all should be honored to meet Mayor Hartsfield in person. That's the good part.

Phillip looked over at me and smiled one of his fakey smiles. He began:

"The Freedom Pledge
I am an American. A free American. . . ."

Phillip was talking like he meant what he was saying about being an American. But I knew better. At the end he gave a little bow. Miss Fowler clapped loudly. Some of the other kids, like BB, clapped too.

I just sat there fuming. Why couldn't I just recite the stupid pledge? Why was I so scared of speaking in front of people? Most of the kids in here I'd known my whole life. 'Course, there'd be a heap more people in Atlanta than there was here in class when it came time to really recite the pledge. Who was I kidding? I couldn't do it.

Now Margo, Phillip, and two other kids led the class in singing the Freedom Train song. They didn't sound nothing like Bing Crosby and the Andrews Sisters. Miss Fowler should've let Joyce Brookshire sing it. Everybody knows she's the best singer in our class.

It didn't matter none, though, 'cause once you heard that song, no matter who was singing it, the chorus stayed stuck in your head all day long.

"Here comes the Freedom Train.
You better hurry down,
Just like a Paul Revere
It's comin' into your hometown."

I bet the man who wrote that song, Irving Berlin,
didn't have no stage fright.

✦ THE THIRD WILLIAM ✦

When school let out that day for Christmas, we run outta there like a stampede in a cowboy movie. Boy, was we glad Jesus was born.

Outside on the front steps Ronnie said, "I got something for you."

"What?" I said.

"An early Christmas present."

"You gonna give it to me now?" I asked.

"You *need* it now. Here," he said, putting something hard and furry in my hand.

I looked at it. It was a rabbit's foot, a gray rabbit's foot.

"My pa got it for me to give to you, straight from

the left-eyed man. It'll bring you some luck. Lord knows you gonna need it."

"Will it keep Phillip Granger from jumping on me again?" I asked.

"I heard he hit you with a plank. He been bragging about it."

"Yeah, he did."

"You okay?"

"I suppose. What'd he say 'bout it?"

"Just that he knocked you out cold and got BB to throw Chester away."

My head shot up. "What?"

"You didn't know. Sorry. That's why I decided not to wait till Christmas to give you your foot. Seems like you need it now."

"He—he—he h-h-hurt Chester?" I could feel tears coming up. I couldn't cry. I just couldn't. People was still walking past us on the steps.

"I don't think they hurt him. BB just said that Phillip made him throw your frog away. Truth was BB said Phillip's scared of frogs. Wouldn't even touch it."

I was so mad I thought the bandage might pop off

my head. He had no call to bother Chester. I balled up my fists.

"Here he comes. Let's get out of here," Ronnie said.

"No, I ain't gonna let him get away with hurting Chester."

"Come on. Don't be stupid. You know you could probably beat Phillip, he's nothing but a tall string-bean bully, but he ain't gonna fight fair, man. Besides, you know BB, he ain't no meany like Phillip. Jimmy Ray told me BB probably just sneaked and let Chester go. So come on."

I shook my head. Phillip Granger had gone too far. He done crossed the line this time.

"Remember what Joseph told you 'bout fighting right. You said you wasn't gonna fight no more."

"Well, Joseph ain't here. Maybe he's wrong about fighting."

"Hey, you," Phillip Granger said. "Ready for your next whupping? Come on. I been looking for you."

A horn blew several times in a row. "Get out here, boy. I'm in a hurry," Mr. Granger shouted. "Hurry up. You wasting my time."

"I'll get you later," Phillip said, hopping down

the stairs, three steps at a time. Then he stopped and looked back at me. "Where's your little froggy, Cl-yyy-yde?"

"Boy, bring yourself on," Mr. Granger yelled.

"Show-off," Ronnie said under his breath. "I told you it would work."

"What?"

"Your lucky rabbit's foot. Come on, let's go home."

Me and Ronnie kicked a can back and forth as we walked. I told him about what had happened to me the day before . . . but I didn't tell him about the colored man and his son, neither. "Can you help me look for Chester? BB could've left him at the roundhouse."

"Can't. Wish I could, but can't. Gotta be straight home from school to help my ma in the store. Pa's out of town. You want to read the new *Archie Comics*? Pa just got it in. You can sneak and read it and bring it to me tomorrow before he gets back."

"Okay," I said, knowing that was Ronnie's way of trying to make me feel better. If his pa found out he'd let me read the comic without paying for it, he'd skin him alive. "I'll walk you home to get it. I'll look for Chester on my way back."

At Ronnie's I stuffed the comic in my pants underneath my shirt so his ma wouldn't see it. The comics cost ten cents and my ma would get me if she knew I spent money for 'em. She thought comics was bad for kids, just like the Salvation Army said.

On the walk back home I slowed down when I got near the roundhouse. I could hear the colored men talking and working. I stopped to search for Chester under some bushes. Maybe BB didn't hurt him. Maybe I'd find him lying underneath some leaves, resting like he likes to do in the daytime.

"Pst. Pst."

When I heard it, my heart froze. I was too scared to even turn around. All my madness was gone from earlier, and I really didn't know if I could win a fight with Phillip now.

"Hey, it's me," I heard the voice say.

I looked around. I didn't see nobody. But some of the fear left me.

"Over here. Walk ten steps right, six steps left, and duck down."

I did what the voice said.

"Hey, I thought it was you."

The Third William stuck out his hand to shake.

He had on some fancy black leather-looking gloves. I wondered if they were real leather. I noticed his clothes and shoes were fancy too. They looked a lot better than my Sunday clothes. He was squatting down. "I'm looking for your frog, what's his name, Chester? What kind of frog is he?"

I squatted down with him. I shook his hand. Whatever the gloves were made of, they were soft and smooth. It felt the same as shaking anybody's hand other than that. I thought, *What made me think it might feel different to shake his hand?* "Thanks. I'm looking for him myself. He's a barking tree frog." Then I told the Third William what BB was supposed to have done, and then what he might've done, knowing BB.

The Third William said, "Yes, when the tall boy started running away, the other boy dropped whatever he had in his hand over here, just before he ran off. Actually, I guessed it might have been your frog. That's why I was looking for him under this clump of bushes. Frogs love damp places."

"I sure hope he is here," I said, trying to sound out my words better. "How you know that? You like 'em too?"

"I'm an amateur herpetologist."

He said it like everybody already knew what "herp-whatever" meant. If it hadn't been for Principal Little, I wouldn't know he was even talking about frogs.

The Third William said, "If we don't find him, I wouldn't worry about him. Tree frogs are resilient."

I just shook my head. Again I didn't know what he was talking about, "resil-" something or another. I couldn't even figure I'd remember the word to look it up or ask anybody about it, since I ain't never heard it before. I busied myself looking for Chester.

There was a long silent time while we searched.

Finally the Third William said, "You excited about getting your American Flyer?"

I wanted to ask him why he talked so proper. But instead I just said, "Yep, been wanting it for a long time. It's the best Christmas present in the world. You?"

"Not really. I'm more excited about going to New York after Christmas. I love New York. My favorite spot is the Empire State Building."

I stopped moving around and stared at him. "You making that up?"

"No. Why would I make that up?"

"I don't know. I suppose the only person I ever

knew from around here went somewhere like that is my brother, Joseph."

"Well, I go to New York at least twice a year. This is the first time we're going in the winter, though. My father has business there. What does your brother do?"

"He's one of the special chosen guards on the Freedom Train."

"You mean the train carrying the documents?"

"Yeah."

"Wow. I bet he's seen a lot of people. I heard the lines have been as many as twenty blocks long. People have been standing in rain, snow, and ice to see the documents. My father told me that they aren't allowing the train's lines to be segregated. If that's true, I'm going when it comes here. I heard that Mayor Hartsfield is not allowing segregated lines here in Atlanta, either."

I didn't want to say I didn't have a clue what he was going on 'bout, so I shook my head and shrugged. I went back to searching for Chester.

"It's getting dark. I'd better make my way home. Would you like to come to my house and play for a while?"

I didn't look up. I wanted to say yeah. Instead I

didn't say nothing. Just stared down at the ground. I didn't know why, but it didn't feel like I should go to his house.

"Never mind," he said, hopping up. He started walking away. "I'll see you around."

I said, "Wait."

He turned around.

"I—I'm sorry," I said. "I just can't go. I gotta go home."

He smiled. "It's okay. Really. I understand."

"You understand what?" I asked him, 'cause for the life of me, I couldn't understand. What was so wrong with me playing with him?

He shrugged and kept walking.

I said, "Hey."

He turned back again. I said, "Be careful. That boy Phillip Granger is mean as a snake."

He nodded and waved bye.

I wanted to run after him and go home and play with his train. Honest, I did, but it was something holding my feet to the spot and shutting off the wind in my throat.

I watched him until he was out of sight. Then I ran all the way home.

———— ✪ ————

I ate supper hardly saying a word. Then I went to bed. When Ma came in, I wanted to ask her why we never even talked to colored people. But I didn't say nothin' about it.

After I'd said all the places Joseph had been and she left the room, I pulled out his letters. Two of 'em was about some colored men. I'd read about 'em, but I didn't understand what Joseph was on about. These colored men were the porters that waited on them on the train. One was named E. B. Long, and even though he was only thirty years old, he was a veteran of the Eighth Air Force. Then there was P. J. Jackson, who was thirty too, and he was a veteran of the French and Belgian fronts, whatever that meant. Ernest Jackson was the oldest at thirty-two, he was a veteran of the India-Burma theater of war. I'd have to ask Joseph did he mean this guy was in the picture show?

And then there was W. C. Lounds, who was the closest to Joseph's age. I reread the letter. It said that this Lounds fellow had become Joseph's best friend. I ain't never heard of a colored man being a white man's best friend, unless I count what Dr. Dobbs said. I wondered if Principal Little would say Dr. Dobbs was his best friend?

Joseph said, now that he and this Lounds was friends, he could see things better. He was on about how sometimes you could see something all your life that was clearly wrong, but you just weren't paying attention to it. I didn't really understand what he was so upset about, so I mostly paid no attention to it the first time I read the letter.

I tried reading all of the letters again, in case I had missed more stuff. But I must've fell asleep, because the next thing I knew, the sun was peeping into the room. I jumped up, dressed, and ate breakfast. I tore up the room trying to find what I was gonna give Ronnie for Christmas. It sure is easy to hide something from yourself. I stuffed Ronnie's present in my pocket. Me and him both had Ovaltine Captain Midnight secret decoder badges, until Phillip took his. Me and Ronnie was like a part of the Secret Squadron, and Phillip was the evil Ivan Shark. Now Ronnie could have mine, since Captain Midnight's badges was his favorite anyway. My favorite was the Wheaties signaling mirror, but Phillip took that, too.

I sat on the porch reading *Archie Comics* #29. I read "Just Plane Trouble" first. Ain't no doubt 'bout it, Veronica's Uncle Bumble sure don't like Archie.

Whilst I was reading, I thought to myself, *Sometimes I feel like Archie. And if Phillip Granger had a guitar, he'd be Reggie Mantle 'cause he's just as bad.*

When I got to the puzzle page, my fingers was itching to fill it out. But I knew that would get Ronnie in trouble, so I went on to reading "Shoot the Works." I couldn't stop laughing. I was thinking, *That Archie gets in so much trouble, and they're mad at me for bringing Chester to school.* I didn't like "Pack Up Your Troubles," and I don't never read the "Hollywood Tattle Tale," 'cause I don't never know who he's talkin' 'bout. I skipped the story "The Sitter," 'cause I didn't really wanna read about babies, and the "Hollywood Quiz" page. All that was left was Betty and Veronica with Mr. Weatherbee and Miss Grundy, who reminds me of Miss Fowler. When I finished reading, I ran to take the comic back so Ronnie wouldn't get in trouble. I squeezed my lucky rabbit's foot on the way, just in case it worked.

★ THE CURE FOR STAGE FRIGHT ★

Christmas vacation is a funny time. In the village we get an extra week out of school on account of the mill's schedule. Us kids spend all our time talking 'bout what we want for Christmas and whether we think we'll get it or not. Sure, we play steelies, red rover, and kick the can. And in the evenings we play spitball. This year I felt good that we got all these days without the likes of Phillip Granger. But mostly we just talk about what we're gonna get.

This year wasn't no different.

Ronnie was sweeping the store porch when I got there. I sneaked him the comic book back and sat down on the step. I waited while he finished his chores.

When he was done, he come outside and sat beside me.

"What was Archie doin'?"

"Same. This time he shot a hole in the school wall with an elephant rifle. He can make you split your gut laughin'."

"Yeah. He stays in more trouble than any of us."

I pulled Ronnie's present out of my pocket and handed it to him.

"No way," he said. "You giving me your badge?"

"Ain't nothin' much. You're a good buddy."

We weren't much for sweet-talking, so Ronnie punched me in the arm and said, "Thanks. Hey, you find Chester?"

"Nope, but I think he's all right." I didn't say because the Third William told me that BB dropped him near the roundhouse.

Ronnie hopped up. "I been thinking, I got some ideas 'bout curing you from being scared of talking in front of people."

"I ain't gonna be speaking in front of no people, remember?"

"It don't matter," Ronnie said. "I ain't done all this thinking for nothin'. We can do it for when you do speak in front of people."

I didn't want to do it. But hey, I had to admit the rabbit's foot seemed to be working, so maybe some other tricks of Ronnie's would too.

First we hunted down a writing spider, which was clinging to a corner in the storeroom window in back of the store. Writing spiders like to spin in the sun, but it ain't easy to find them when it gets real cold. Good thing there hadn't been a freeze, or we would've been lookin' all day. "Now what?" I asked him.

"You keep it till you get ready to speak."

"Then?"

"Then you take it out and hold it in your hand. See, I done figured on account of you being so nervous you can't remember the words. That's why you're stuttering."

"Ronnie, how's the writing spider gonna help? Is it gonna write out the words for me?"

"Naw, don't be stupid. I think if you hold the writing spider in your hand, just before you get ready to speak it'll bring you good luck, 'cause you know the words is in the spider and he remembers them. Get it?"

"There's one big problem," I said. "Writing spiders' webs might look like writing, but it ain't."

"But maybe it's writing only what spiders under-stand. Thought of that? Just do it. What you got to lose?"

I wasn't too keen on holding the spider in my hand, but Ronnie insisted. "Now what?"

"Practice. Start saying the pledge," he said, like I should've already known what to do next. "Go on."

"All right already." I cleared my throat.

"The Freedom Pledge
I-I-I am an Am-m-m-m-merican.
A fr-fr-free American."

"No wait! Wait!" Ronnie yelled. "You gotta put your hand over your mouth. What's wrong with ya? The spider can see you plain as day whilst you hold-ing him up like that."

"So?"

"You can't let the spider count your teeth, 'cause you know if he counts your teeth, you gonna die."

I just stood there looking at him. "What?"

"Trust me, just go on. I know it'll work. Say the pledge, put the spider in your right hand—that'll make it seem better—and keep your left hand over your mouth while you do it."

I shook my head and started over. But even with the writing spider crawling in my right hand and my left hand covering up my teeth, I was still stuttering.

I couldn't take no more. I said, "Ronnie, don't you get it? I can't say this pledge right even in front of you and a stupid spider."

"Don't worry. I got other ideas. Now, on to the second part. You know stuff like this gotta be in threes."

"Stuff like what?"

"You know. Magic stuff. Come on."

"Where to now?" I asked, letting the spider go free. I wasn't even believing I was going on with this.

"Butterflies, Clyde. You know how you always say you feel like you got butterflies in your stomach and you gonna throw up?"

"Yeah," I said, waiting to see if this could get any weirder.

"All we need is to put some butterflies in a jar, and then just before you get ready to talk, you look at them and you see, 'Hey, they ain't really in my stomach.'"

"Yeah, well, it's winter, there ain't no butterflies."

"Then, we use a substitute, maybe moths or some other kind of flying bugs might do."

"It's dead cold out here. Ain't no bugs."

"Okay then, we'll move on. We save that for if'n you ever have to speak in the spring or summer."

I squeezed my eyes shut. Shook my head. It could get weirder. "And my throwing up?"

He smiled. "That's the easiest one of all, that's why it's tied into number two instead of having a part on its own."

"Okay," I said, sighing. "Tell me."

"You throw up all you got in you before you speak," he said, shrugging.

"You want me to just start throwing up. Gee whiz."

"It's easy. I do it all the time when I don't want to go to school. You just stick your finger down your throat like this," he said, demonstrating.

I jumped back. "You're crazy. I ain't throwing up. And don't you throw up neither."

"Awright," he said, pulling his finger out of his mouth. "On to number three. The last part give me the most trouble. At first I was thinking we could get a chunk of ice when the ice truck come by and wrap it inside something and put it around your neck to keep the sweat down. But then I remembered you said you wasn't sweating 'cause you was hot. So that's when I come up with the best idea of all."

I dropped my head. "All right, let's hear it."

"We gonna find somebody with a baby. Maybe Mrs. Irene up on Carroll Street. We gonna borrow some of her baby's diapers. They got money, so they're using the real high-priced diapers from a store. We wrap them diapers all around your neck and chest so they soak up the sweat, same as they soak up a baby's pee." He wiped his hands, he was done. "See? Clever, ain't it?" Ronnie said, grinning.

I wanted to say, "'Bout as clever as kids saying 'Whoo, whoo'" but I couldn't hurt his feelings like that. He was my best buddy. And he was trying to help. So I said, "Okay. If I make up my mind to do it, and Miss Fowler lets me, which I don't think she will 'cause she's already given the pledge to Phillip to say, then I'll try to use your plan."

"It's gonna work. Trust me."

The bottom line was I did trust him. Not his plan, but him for sure.

———— ✪ ————

The next few days me and Ronnie steered clear
of Phillip. We played games, wrestled, read comic
books, shot steelie rollers, and talked about what it
was gonna be like to see Joseph standing guard at the
Freedom Train. Ronnie thought I should sell Joseph's
autograph on slips of paper to kids in the village so
we could make some money. I knew Joseph wouldn't
go for it, but I said I'd think about it.

The day before Christmas Eve we were sitting on
the steps trying to make a three-rock slingshot. We
weren't making much success. That made me think
about the Third William even harder. I asked Ronnie,
like it was an easy question, "Have you ever played
with a colored boy?"

"Who told you that?" he said, jumping up. "That
ain't so. I wasn't playing with him."

"Calm down," I said. "Why you got your britches
all in a bunch? I was just asking, that's all."

Ronnie sat back down and dropped his head. "I
don't want to talk about it."

"About what it?" I asked.

Ronnie looked around like he was getting ready to

change into Superman's outfit. "You really ain't hear about it?"

"Hear about what?"

"Last summer," he said, looking around again like he was stealing. "You know that colored woman who helps my ma out on Saturdays?

"I've seen her a time or two. You got in trouble for playing with y'all's maid?"

"Don't be silly. I was playing with her son. We was just playing marbles. You should've seen them. He had three tiger eyes."

"So, what's wrong with that? You can get that many tiger eyes if you got the money for 'em or you make good trades."

"The marbles ain't the big stink."

"I ain't following you," I said. "What caused a stink?"

"Old man Ricker and his sons come to buy some tobacco."

I frowned. "That's the stink? Old man Ricker always lets his boys chew tobacco."

"No, when they come out of the store, one of the Ricker boys stoops down and says, 'You playing with this here boy, Ronnie?'

"The boy, I can't even remember his name now, just looked at me and shook his head no. But I said, 'Yeah, we playing marbles. I wish they was mine but they his.'

"Then the Ricker boy scoops all the marbles in his hand and stands up.

"I said, 'What are you doing?'

"Old man Ricker says, 'He's claiming them marbles. You ought to know better than to play with that boy. He sure ought to know better than to play with you, so he must not want them marbles.'

"About that time my pa comes out. He says, 'What's going on out here?'

"Maybell's boy is crying, but he ain't saying nothing. I said, 'They took his marbles.'

"Pa says, 'That boy's father been saving those marbles up for years for the boy, before he was even born. I know 'cause I sold them to him. So go on, Ricker, give 'em back.'

"Old man Ricker says, 'My boy says they his. They his. You want me to call the law? What you think they gonna say when it's my word against a Negra boy? Maybe this will teach your son and that boy a lesson.'

"My pa says, 'Come on, Ricker. Give the boy his marbles back. His daddy's dead now.'

"'Good,' Mr. Ricker says. 'I bet he'll think twice about who he plays with from now on.'

"Pa says, 'That's enough, Ricker. Just get on out of here.'

"Right after, Pa tells Maybell it's best she don't bring her son back no more. And from then on he walks Maybell to the edge of Cabbagetown to make sure don't nobody bother her."

I swallowed hard. "You mean they got that mad just 'cause you was playing marbles with him?"

I must have looked as puzzled as I felt, 'cause Ronnie said, "Yeah. I still don't know what was so wrong about it. But Pa told me that if he'da let Ricker call the police, it might have been even worse on the boy."

"What's that mean?" I asked him.

Ronnie shook his head. "That it ain't safe around here to be playing with the coloreds, that's what it means, Clyde. Now, can we talk about something else, before I get in more trouble?"

After hearing what happened to Ronnie, I decided it was best to never mention the Third William to anyone. It wasn't 'cause I didn't like him or nothing. It just was for the best.

★ CHRISTMAS EVE ★

Come Christmas Eve we always go shop for presents in downtown Atlanta, mainly 'cause my folks save money till the last minute so it adds up. Ma keeps the savings in a coffee can on top of the kerosene cooking stove. Pa says it ain't safe up there on account of the heat. In the mill village there's a fire every week started by somebody's cooking stove. But Ma always says, "A habit is harder to break than steel."

We dressed up. I put on my Sunday clothes and my penny loafers. I was wearing my good wool toboggan hat, not the ripped one. I tried not to act too excited, but I surely was.

We don't go to town much. The village has its own stores: the Red Dot store; J. M. Little's Grocery; no kin to Ronnie, the general store that sells medicine, dry goods, pants, and shirts. When we buy meat, we walk to the meat market on Auburn. So going into downtown Atlanta is a big deal that only happens once a year.

Ma put on her best dress and a little hat on top of her curly black hair. She looked real purty. Her gray coat had seen better days, but it was warm looking. Pa, he just kept on his working clothes—his overalls, a short wool coat, and brogans. We all rode the trolley down Auburn to Peachtree Street.

This morning when I seen Pa counting out bills and change from the can, I felt maybe I was close to really getting my American Flyer. Maybe it was finally gonna happen. I wanted to see it up on a table like the Third William's train. The kitchen table wasn't big enough to hold it. And Ma wouldn't let me use the eating table for it nohow. Maybe Pa would help me build something to sit the train on. He was right good with his hands. If Joseph was home, I know he'd build it for me. It's times like these I miss him bad. . . .

When we got off the trolley, Pa said he was gonna give me and Ma a special treat. We followed behind him till he stopped in front of the Rich's store.

I ain't never been inside Rich's Department Store before. Ain't had no call. Ma always said we couldn't even afford a handkerchief from there.

Ma said, "What on earth are you doing?"

"We gonna go in here, and I'm gonna buy my wife and son some food up in that tea place restaurant for Christmas."

"Lord, I'm not dressed to go in the Magnolia Room. We can't afford it, Jim. We couldn't have went in there when you was working full-time. It's all right. Let's go."

Pa frowned. "Why'd you gotta bring up I ain't working full-time? Things 'bout to change around here. I heard some of the men is 'bout fed up with the coloreds taking our jobs at the railroad. So don't think I'll be half-time for much longer. Anyhow, I want you to have a nice Christmas gift, Lila. You deserve it."

"But I ain't dressed proper," Ma said, fretting.

I said, "You look real nice, Ma." That part was the truth, but I was also figuring the sooner we ate, the sooner I got my American Flyer.

"All right, then," Ma said.

Pa opened that door, and all three of us walked

into Rich's Department Store like we might be the owners of it.

I ain't never seen so much shiny stuff. It smelled real good too, like a bunch of flowers all smashed together.

Ma said, "Jim, is it all right if I just take a look at some of that perfume over yonder?"

Pa nodded his head. I sort of felt proud of him. It weren't like Pa to come into no place like this. This was just for Ma.

She walked over to the counter and picked up one of the bottles that had TESTER written on it. A woman with a ton of face paint come up and snatched it out of Ma's hand. "May I help you," she said, sounding like it was the last thing she wanted to do.

Ma said, "No, ma'am. I'm just looking."

The woman said, "This bottle sells for thirty-five dollars."

I said, "Naw, it says 'tester' right on it. Don't that mean you can just try it out?"

Pa said, "Hush up, boy. Let's go on upstairs."

Ma nodded to the woman and turned to Pa. She give him a look, but I wasn't sure what it meant. We walked over to the elevator. There was a fancy-dressed man sitting in it. He opened the door wide so we could get on. "What floor, *please*?" he said with sort of a smirk on his face. There was three more people on there with us. They gave their floors.

Pa said, "I don't rightly know. We want to go to that tea restaurant."

He shut the door and we went up.

"Here we are. You folks have a good day," the man said, nodding that we should get off on the sixth floor. When we walked away, I heard the people and the man laughing 'bout something. I turned around to see what was funny. One of them was pointing at Ma's shoes.

I looked down at them. They didn't look funny to me. A little crooked on the heel, but they was okay.

When we got to the tearoom, another fancy woman asked if we had something called a reservation.

Pa said, "No, ma'am, I don't reckon so. We just come for a bite to eat."

The woman smiled a tight kind of smile, and said, "Well, without a reservation you'll have to wait."

Pa said, "That's fine."

She walked away, taking a few looks back at us. She went over to another woman and whispered something. That woman looked at us and then turned away real quick.

We stood there waiting, watching folk go past us to be seated at tables. I ain't heard the woman asking nobody else for that reserva-whatever-it-was. I started thinking maybe this wasn't such a good idea. Finally the woman come over and said, "Follow me." She sat us near the swinging doors for the kitchen part.

Ma was loving it. I knew 'cause sometimes I'd hear her talking to one of her friends about one day going to this tea place and sitting down at a table.

The table had a white, lacy tablecloth on it, real flowers, and some lit candles even though it was daytime. All the tables were like this one. The napkins was even made out of lacy cloth.

It seemed like a long time before anybody even noticed we was sitting there. I was looking at the people around the room. All the men had on suits. Most of the women had on hats and gloves. I thought, *Why they got on gloves in here where it's warm?* But 'bout that time a waitress come up to us.

"What would you like to order?"

Ma looked from me to Pa. We were stumped.

None of us knew exactly what to do. We had never been in a restaurant before, just the soda fountain at the drugstore.

"We'll have some of that there tea," Pa said, pointing to a man near us drinking from a fancy cup, "for my wife and boy. And give them some of those little square cakes over yonder to go with it. I just want water. Thank you, ma'am."

Me and Ma drank our tea and eat them cakes without hardly saying a word. I didn't feel so great about this place. People kept staring at us like we was the monkeys at a show.

I was so glad when Pa said, "We best be getting on to W. T. Grant's so you can get your present, boy."

Outside Ma give Pa a little peck on the cheek. He smiled. I'd never seen Pa or Ma smooching out in the open before. It give me the heebies.

We got to W. T. Grant's in no time. My stomach was in knots. I wondered what magic cure Ronnie would come up with. Probably tie a knotted rope around my stomach or something and hang me out a window.

Pa was in the lead, and we went straight to where the toys was. The American Flyer 464 was on a big table. There it was, the Hudson 464, developed, it said, at the Gilbert Hall of Science. The writing said: "Here for the first time are the trains every scale model railroader has wanted, trains that puff real smoke . . . trains that reproduce the throbbing *choo-choo* sounds of a giant locomotive."

On the display they had fake mountains and tunnels for the train to go through. There was even fake people working on the tracks. I couldn't believe it, but I was about to have the train of my dreams.

I read the big sign over the table: SEE 'EM PUFF SMOKE, HEAR 'EM CHOO-CHOO. Underneath where the price tag had been—it was gone. The train cost was a blank space and now the sign said it was only available as a set.

Pa said, "I better get a clerk."

When he come back, he looked like he'd been run over by a train.

"Son . . . ," he said.

And before he went on, I knew I wasn't gonna get the American Flyer. Pa, he ain't a man of flowery words. He's plainspoken, as Ma calls it. He calls me his boy most of the time. But sometimes he calls me son, and it ain't usually good news that comes after.

"I ain't got enough for that American Flyer. The salesclerk says they only have this one left, and you gotta buy the full dang thing. Even if it were another one by itself, it sounds like I might not of had enough money. They went up on the price of all the trains on account of everybody buying 'em 'cause of the Freedom Train coming here right after Christmas."

Darn Freedom Train. Made me mad enough to puff smoke of my own.

Pa said, "But I got enough for you to pick out a good pair of skates or even a scooter if you want it."

"What about a BB gun? A Daisy pump Red Ryder?" I asked, excited.

Ma didn't say a word. She just cleared her throat.

Pa said, "No BB gun. You like scooters, don't you?"

I wanted to say I didn't really want no scooter, but I just nodded my head. I done learned from Ma not to look a gift horse in the mouth.

I said, "Sure, Pa. I want a scooter." I walked to where the scooters was. I spotted one that was red, white, and blue and had a flag on the side. But by now I didn't want nothin' that reminded me of that

Freedom Train. "I reckon this one," I said, picking up the tag of a green scooter with a yellow lightning strike running down its side.

Pa looked at the tag. He nodded his head. "All right. Bring it on."

I toted it to the cash register, and Pa paid for it with bills and change.

I ain't gonna lie, I was disappointed. Just once I wanted to get exactly what I asked for at Christmas.

We rode back home on the trolley, me hugging my scooter like I thought the other people might steal it. By the time we walked up toward our house, I was feeling pretty good, pushing along on my brand-new scooter. I didn't never put both my feet to glide on it. I wanted to save it for Christmas.

Then Pa stopped in his tracks. Me and Ma stopped too. Mr. Granger and Phillip was leaning on their car, waiting out in front of our house.

Ma squeezed my hand. "Come on, son."

I didn't know what to think. Did Phillip tell his Pa a lie on me? Was he here to let Ma go from her job?

Pa said, "Come on. Let's see what they want."

⋆ MEN'S TALK ⋆

"Howdy, folks," Mr. Granger said.

Ma said, "Howdy," then she poked me in the side. She didn't poke Pa.

I said, "Hey."

"I'm sorry to barge in on you on Christmas Eve, Mr. Thomason," Mr. Granger said, "but I just need a few minutes of your time."

Ma said, "You want to come inside, Mr. Granger?"

"No, thank you, Lila," Mr. Granger said.

I wondered why Mr. Granger called her Lila and not Mrs. Thomason, but she called him Mr. Granger.

"This visit is men's talk," Mr. Granger said, like he could run Ma off her own place.

Pa nodded to Ma, and she went in the house. I stood beside Pa.

"What can I do for you?" Pa said.

"It's what I can do for you. I'm a member of a group called the Columbians. We're a few decent men trying to protect the rights of our own," Mr. Granger said. He looked at Phillip. "Go on, talk with your buddy, while his daddy and I talk."

I couldn't believe Mr. Granger thought me and his son were buddies. More like sworn enemies. I don't suppose he told his pa that he hit me in the head with a plank only a few days before.

"Go on, now, boy. What'd I tell you," Mr. Granger said, shoving Phillip hard on the shoulder. He darn near knocked him over.

"Okay, Daddy," Phillip said. "But I'm—"

"Shut up and do what I say," Mr. Granger said, sounding mad as a rabid dog. "You want me to smack you one, boy?"

"No, sir," Phillip said, dropping his head down like it might've weighed too much.

My pa looked at me and nodded. "Go on, talk to him, son."

I put my scooter down careful like so it wouldn't

get scratched or nothin'. Me and Phillip took a few steps away from Pa and Mr. Granger.

Phillip said, "My daddy says we gotta be friends now."

All the bully meanness usually in his face was gone. He almost looked like a regular human. I still acted like he'd said he wanted one of my arms. I said, "You know good and well we ain't friends."

"I know. But that's how it's gotta be," he said. "Me and you, 'cause we got men's work to do now."

I was still looking at him like he was from Mars. What made him think we could be friends now? "I ain't feeble," I said. "You sucker punched me with a plank."

"Shhhh. I'm sorry, okay? Look, all I know is, if I don't want no beating, I gotta be friends with you. 'Cause we both got men's work to do with my old man."

"What are you going on 'bout?" I said. "What men's work?"

"Your daddy will tell you," he said, sticking out his hand. "Shake? Friends?"

I looked over at his daddy. Whatever he was telling my pa, he was mad about it. Real mad. Maybe if

I didn't shake, he'd be mad at my ma, too. I shook. But I didn't mean it. After that we just stood there looking at each other.

A few minutes later his daddy said, "Let's go," and opened his car door.

Phillip shrugged at me. "See you."

Before he could've even moved, his daddy said, "You hear me, boy? Get in the damn car, I ain't got all night."

Then something terrible happened; I was feeling sorry for Phillip Granger. My pa ain't no softy, but he ain't mean, neither. Mr. Granger was just a downright hateful man. And it seemed like he didn't even want to know Phillip, let alone be his daddy.

Just before he closed the car door, I heard Mr. Granger say, "You know damn well I don't want to be in Cabbagetown after dark. It ain't safe over here with all this poor white trash."

I looked up at Pa. "What's he mean, Pa? Is he meaning us, we're like trash?" I asked.

"Don't pay that no mind, son. Sticks and stones son. Sticks and stones."

When we got inside, Ma had put supper on the table. "I had a very nice day, Papa," she said, smiling.

Ma didn't call Pa sweet names, but when she did, she called him Papa.

Pa grinned and sat down at the table. He grabbed a biscuit and some butter.

I said, "So, what's the men's stuff we gonna be doing, Pa?"

He bit his biscuit. "Eat your food, Clyde. Then you can go out and ride your scooter for a spell. And we got a surprise for you in the morning."

Ma said, "That's right. You got another present comin'."

I said, "Thank you, Ma and Pa. Thank you for the scooter."

After supper I rode my scooter to Ronnie's, even though I'd meant to save it for Christmas morning. But he wasn't home. Sometimes he and his family went to his grandma's for Christmas. They never gave him no warning 'bout their plans. We was used to it.

★ GIRLS, FROGS, AND FRIENDS ★

I come back to the village from Ronnie's, kicking with my right foot and gliding far as I could on the dirt. All the main stores is on Carroll Street, including the barbershop, not that I ever been in. But by now the stores was closed. I didn't see no kids out, except Joyce Brookshire sitting on her porch, strumming a guitar.

"Hey, Clyde," she said. "That what you got for Christmas?"

Every kid in the mill village already knows what toys you got, so it ain't hard to spot new ones. "You get that guitar?" I said, gliding over to her.

"Yep. It plays good."

I could see her teeth. She had the best teeth of any of us kids in the village. Her skin was kinda dark like

94

an Indian, not that I'd seen a real Indian before, and she had long, long black eyelashes. We been knowing each other since we went to the mill's kindergarten together.

Her long black hair was down around her shoulders. I ain't never seen her without her pigtails. "What happened to your hair?"

"My ma fixed it. She says I'm getting old enough not to wear pigtails. I kind of like my pigtails best, though, 'cause they don't never get in my way."

"Yeah, I see what you mean," I said as her hair fell down over the guitar strings. I watched her pulling it back off her face. For some reason I felt kind of funny inside watching her, so I said, "What you doing tomorrow?"

"Nothin' but go to church," she said. "You going?"

Most of the people who go to church in the village go to the Salvation Army church just a few houses down from Joyce's house.

"I reckon we ain't going to church. Ma's gonna stay home to fix a big supper with a hen for Pa. And she says they got another Christmas surprise for me."

"Your train?" Joyce said.

"Naw. I ain't gonna get the train. Price done went up, thanks to the dad-blasted Freedom Train coming to town. Seem like to me if more people was buying the train, the price should've gone down—not up."

"Yeah. My ma says that's the way things is. We can't wait to see the Freedom Train. We want to see the Bill of Rights."

I frowned. "I don't care nothin' 'bout seeing none of it."

"You gonna get to see your brother, though," Joyce said.

"Yeah, sure, I wanna see him, just don't care 'bout the train."

"I bet he's gonna be disappointed you ain't reciting the pledge."

"I bet he don't care."

"Bet he does. My ma says that it ain't right that somebody like the Grangers gets the money. They got plenty of money already. And they don't care 'bout nobody's rights."

"I don't care neither," I said.

"Yeah. I can see you don't," Joyce said, getting up.

"You like the folk my ma's always telling me 'bout."

"What folk?"

"One of them folk. Folk who think it's everybody else's job to say something. That's why women at the mill is treated so bad. Won't nobody but a few of them speak up. If they'd all do it together, folk would have to listen."

Folk in the village said Joyce's ma was either a troublemaker or a fool. She was always fussing 'bout something. I was kind of scared of her. The Brookshires weren't known for taking no mess. Joyce was the only person at school Phillip Granger didn't mess with. I bet Joyce and her ma and sisters would beat Phillip Granger to a pulp if he tangled with her.

Joyce walked into her house and slammed the door behind her. She just left me sitting on the porch. Girls.

I got on my scooter and went home. When I got there, Ma said I had a visitor.

"Ronnie's back?"

"Nope. It was your principal, Mr. Little. He brought this box here for you. And this here letter."

I took the letter and the box. It had holes punched in the top. I unfolded the letter:

Clyde,

Dr. Dobbs told me you lost your friend
Chester. So he asked me to get this one for
you for Christmas from him and William III. I
hope you like him. Have a good Christmas.

Mr. Leon Little

Inside the box was a barking tree frog.

I was fighting back tears.

Ma said, "What's the matter? What does it say?"

I folded the letter up. "Just that Mr. Little got me a
frog 'cause I told him at school that I lost Chester."

I wanted to tell her the truth about Dr. Dobbs and
the Third William, but I didn't. In the back of my
mind all I could see was the Rickers. I took the frog
into my room and closed the door. I sat on the bed,
rubbing the frog's back. I had to give him a name. I
named him the Second Chester and asked God, wherever the First Chester was, if he'd keep him safe.

★ MEN'S WORK NEVER TAKES A HOLIDAY ★

Before dawn I was wide awake. I wanted the surprise Ma and Pa said they had for me. We didn't have a tree. Pa said ain't make no sense to kill a tree just to drag it inside a house for a few days. So Ma fixed a little crate with a nice cloth over it in the corner with our Christmas presents on it.

Ma and Pa got up, wiping sleep outta their eyes. Ma said, "You wanna open your present first?"

"Naw, you and Pa open yours first." Ronnie had given me one of them little glass figures that you sat up on the table for Ma. It wasn't new but it looked new. He said his Ma had thrown it out. I traded him one of my tiger eyes for it. I give Pa the cordovan brown shoe polish that Joseph sent me. It's what the

guards on the train spit-shine their shoes with. Ma
and Pa both knew I didn't have no money to buy a
new present.

"This is right perty," Ma said.

"Sure is," Pa said. "And I can spit-shine my shoes
like your brother's now. Thank you, son."

Ma said, "You're a good boy. Now you open
yours."

I shook my head and grabbed the box. It wasn't
no Gene Autry watch, like I had guessed. I knew
it weren't no train because of the size of the box. I
ripped off the paper.

It had a letter on top of white thin paper. I read it
out loud.

"Dear Clyde,

Merry Christmas. I know Pa's getting you a
train, so I got you this so when you get up
there to say the Freedom Pledge by heart,
you'll be warm. I know how you used to
be scared to talk in a crowd. I knew you'd
outgrow that. I'll feel so proud when I see
you up there on stage. You'll be in good

company with Mayor Hartsfield. He took a brave stand in the South, going against other southern mayors to make sure the whites and coloreds don't have to stand in separate lines. After reading over these documents on the train day after day, I see that's what this country is supposed to be all about, justice and freedom for all. Sometimes, though, it just ain't. My friend W.C., the porter I told you about, gave me this poem. Read it. It's by the Negro poet Langston Hughes, and you'll see what I mean. It's people like us gotta change this. I hope you're still writing in your journal. Save your fifty-dollar prize for college.

Sincerely,
Your brother, Joseph"

Pa said, "Sometimes I think the war rattled that boy's head. What's he on about them coloreds for? If he keeps talking like that, he's gonna get in a heap of trouble."

Ma patted the back of Pa's hand.

"You want me to read the poem?" I asked. The poem was written on more than one sheet of paper, and to be honest I didn't want to read it. I wanted to get to my present. I almost smiled when Ma spoke.

"That's all right," Ma said. "Go on, Clyde, finish opening your present."

I pulled back the white paper. It was a black leather bomber jacket. I ain't never had a jacket this nice. I took it out and held it up.

Pa whistled. "Boy, that cost a pretty penny."

Ma said, "That's mighty nice. Try it on."

I checked the tag in the collar. It said GENUINE LEATHER. I put it on.

"It fits mighty good too," Ma said. "You gonna look so nice up there on that stage."

I wasn't feeling happy like I should've been. Everything was going wrong. I had been too ashamed to tell Ma and Pa that I wasn't reciting the Freedom Pledge. And now, just as Joyce Brookshire bet, Joseph did care 'bout me saying the pledge. I felt like crying. But I knew Pa didn't like no boys crying, so I said, "I gotta go outside and catch a few worms for the Second Chester."

I ran out.

When I got out there, I went on the side of the house and dug for a few grub worms. But while I dug, I let the tears come on out.

After a minute I wiped off my face with my sleeve and went back inside the house. "I gotta give the Second Chester his worms," I said, picking up Joseph's letter. I give the Second Chester the worms and folded up Joseph's letter along with the poem. I put it in my box underneath the bed. I didn't want to think about what Joseph had said in the letter. Not right then. I wanted to enjoy my jacket. I heard Pa calling for me. I went back into the front room.

"See what your ma got me?" Pa said. It was a pack of socks.

"They look good, Pa."

Ma said, "Look what Papa got me."

I smiled. Pa had got her a new pair of shoes. For a second I could almost see the folk on the elevator laughing. I wished Pa would've given 'em to her yesterday to wear to the Rich's store. But it was too late. Just like it was too late for me to make my family proud by saying the Freedom Pledge, unless I could talk Phillip Granger, my new "friend," into letting me say it instead of him. The problem was

I wasn't gonna see Phillip Granger until January 1.

Ma fixed supper. Me and Pa played checkers. He let me beat him some, but I couldn't outplay him fair and square.

When we sat down to eat supper, I could tell something was wrong. Ma was acting like she does whenever Joseph comes home and it's time for him to leave.

The chicken was so good. I was licking my fingers when Ma let on to Pa what was bothering her.

"It ain't right, you know. And it ain't right for you to take the boy."

I wanted to say, "Take me where?" but you don't talk in grown folk's business. So I waited to hear where I was going.

"This is Christmas Day," Ma said. "This don't seem right Christian to me. Granger ain't never even give you so much as a howdy-do till yesterday. Why you think he come here to us?"

"Them Columbians, they's Christian. You always on me 'bout church," Pa said. "Granger is a deacon, and the preacher is part of it too. They say they done warned 'em to move out. What you want me to do? Be the only one from the railroad that don't go? Others here in the village goin'. Ain't just me."

"The Columbians, huh. Them the same ones who blackjacked a Negro man for walking on the street just 'cause they wanted to. And they bombed a poor old Negro woman's house 'cause she moved too close to a white neighborhood."

"You don't know that's what they done," Pa said. "That's just what people said in the newspaper."

Ma looked like she was going to cry. "It ain't right and you know it. Even the police chief says he's gonna get rid of the Klan that's on the police force. But I know why Granger come to us. Ain't nothin' new. They's always putting the poor, the for'ner people, and the Negro people at each other while they's gettin' rich."

"Don't you care, woman, that the coloreds is taking our jobs?"

"What jobs? The mill don't hire 'em. And the railroad just hires 'em to do jobs nobody else wants to do."

"That's enough, now," Pa said. "I'm going."

"At least you could wait till after Christmas."

"I ain't pick Christmas. I don't wanta do it today. But Christmas is the only time all us is off. You know that as well as me."

"It still ain't right."

Pa said, "Ain't no need you getting on about it. What's done is done. I give my word."

I stopped listening. I didn't care 'bout going nowhere with old man Granger and some preacher. This was one argument I hoped Ma would've won. But the truth was, she didn't win many of 'em. For some reason I thought about what Joyce Brookshire said to me about the women at the mill being treated so bad.

When we was done eating, I went to show off my jacket. But wasn't nobody outside playing. It was that way especially when Christmas fell on a Sunday in the village. Lots of people finally had enough time off to visit their kinfolk. Cabbagetown could be like a ghost town on Sundays most times anyway. Everybody was either too tired to come out, too cold, too hot, or working. The mill took up people's entire lives. Joseph said that's why he didn't want me to end up workin' there like Ma and Pa. Joseph was happier than Pa when he finally left the mill and took the railroad job.

Joseph said the mill bosses treated the people like orphaned children. He said they should pay the people more. They barely made enough money to eat, while the owners were sitting somewhere getting rich off of 'em. Joseph was full of talk like that. If Joyce Brookshire was older, she'd make a good sweetheart for Joseph. But picturing Joyce with Joseph made a little pang come on in my stomach. I pushed the thought out of my mind.

I went back in the house. Only Ma was in the kitchen. I went to see 'bout the Second Chester. I said, "I hope the First Chester is faring all right, don't you, buddy?" The Second Chester didn't say a word, but I knew he was thinking on it too.

I knelt down to get my box of letters. The box was gone from under my bed. I checked under my pillow. My journal, my only Superman comic, and my two Batman comics were still there, plus my Lana Turner news picture.

I went in the kitchen. "Ma, somebody done moved my box of letters." I knew it had to be her, but I weren't brave enough to accuse her of taking it.

"Ain't nobody took it. I got it in here," she said, reaching in the cupboard. Some of the papers was on top.

Ma said, "I remembered when you read Joseph's last letter before, you said something about he had put in a poem by a colored man. I just wanted to look at it. I didn't even know colored people was writers."

I picked up the papers and looked at the pages. Ma sometimes just sat looking at the Bible even though she couldn't read it. I reckon that's why she wanted to have a look at the poem.

Ma said, "I wish I could read that poem."

The poem was long. I hoped Ma didn't want me to read it to her. I usually read Ma and Pa Joseph's letters but left out any parts I thought would upset 'em. I didn't read much of the letter to 'em about the colored porters. I thought they'd pay no attention and forget about the poem written by a colored man. Now I wondered if I should have at least read the parts about the porters to Ma.

Before I could decide, Ma tousled my hair and walked to her room.

I took the box back into my room and stuck it back under my bed. I run my hands over my jacket. Smelled the leather. I was 'bout to put it on again when Pa come to my door.

"Let's go, son," he said. "Don't wear your new jacket, put on your old one. And put your old wool toboggan on your head, it's cold out."

I didn't ask him where we was going. My pa didn't like a lot of questions shot at him.

I put on my coat and toboggan. He was waiting for me outside on the porch. I was surprised to see some of the other men from the mill village was out there waiting too.

I whispered to Pa, "Where we going?"

Pa didn't say a word. He just said, "Let's get this over with."

One of the other men said to me, "I'll tell you, son. We going to do men's work. We can't let the coloreds get out of hand."

I looked at Pa, and he looked like he did the whole time Joseph was away fighting in the war—sad.

★ THIS DON'T SEEM LIKE NO MEN'S WORK TO ME ★

We walked to the other side of the tracks, near the roundhouse. It was quiet. Real quiet. The mill shut down all day on Christmas, and this was the first I noticed all the clanging and hissing noises was missing from the air. I thought about Joseph's words, how sometimes something can be there but you just ain't paid it no mind.

Up ahead Phillip and Mr. Granger was standing up on the back of a truck with three other men and two other boys who looked to be 'bout me and Phillip's age.

Another truck come up, spewing dust, with more men on it, including Mr. Ricker and his boys.

The minute I saw the Rickers, I thought about

Ronnie and what they'd done. Wherever the Rickers were there was trouble.

Then another truck pulled up.

My pa knew the second truck of men, they worked with him on the railroad.

Mr. Granger shouted from the bed of one of the trucks, "We come here tonight to do the Lord's bidding and claim our Christian rights. So let's hear from the reverend first."

The man moved in front of Mr. Granger. When he started talking, he was loud and clear. I thought he didn't look scared to speak in front of all us strangers. Why couldn't I be brave like that?

"Brothers, tonight the Lord Jesus Christ, our Savior, calls on us to do his work. How many of you are with us?"

All the men and the boys raised their hands. I put mine up even though I didn't know what he was meaning.

"Good. You understand what is at stake. These Nigras are trying to take our jobs, our houses, and next it will be our womenfolk."

"Yeah, tell it," one of the men yelled.

"We've given this man and his family fair warning.

If we let this one colored family move in on us, the rest of 'em will follow. So now we gonna have to take action."

I was lost. I couldn't figure out what he was talking about, but the way everyone was acting, I was the only one who didn't know.

"How many of you lost your jobs on account of the coloreds at the railroad?" he shouted.

The railroad men nodded their heads and yelled, "Me." Pa didn't say nothin'.

I watched the men's faces. I looked from man to man. They was all looking like they was getting ready to go hunting. I couldn't figure it out.

Then Mr. Granger got up front again. "We been able to hold them off working in the cotton mill, but it ain't gonna be long before they gonna be demanding our jobs. We should've done something when the women come. But we set back and let it happen. Now they's there and we can't get rid of 'em. I say we stop all this madness now. We might not be able to get the women out, but we can sure keep the blacks out."

More men shouted yes. I thought about Ma. She wouldn't want to hear all this meanness. She'd say they all ought be ashamed running down folk. I understood better now why Ma was upset. She wouldn't think this was men's work, not one bit.

The men sort of looked like they were having fun, but also mad. I was feeling confused when Pa put his hand on my shoulder.

I looked up at him. Pa loved us, but he wasn't much for showing it. He looked a lot older than he had at supper.

Mr. Granger said, "Well, let's go do this. If you don't, they'll be coming for your daughters next."

I couldn't help thinking Pa ain't got no daughters.

We all piled onto the trucks. Hayride come to mind, but deep down I knew that weren't it. There was something ugly about this men's work. I could feel it inside. I had the same butterflies and throw-up feeling I get when I'm gonna speak in front of people. I thought about Ronnie and wondered if I had a jar of butterflies, if it would help me. Pa squeezed my shoulder tightly now. And I tell you, for some reason that made me scared.

We didn't go far, just to the center of Reynoldstown. I knew the place. About four white men were standing in a yard talking to a colored man, a woman, and a boy. All at once I couldn't catch my breath. It was the Third William's house.

Everyone hopped off the trucks. Me too.

Mr. Granger handed each man a shovel or a stick. "Come on, men," Mr. Granger said.

Some of the other men had rifles. Two of 'em had torches. We all walked up on the circle of people. I saw another man with a cross hanging from his neck.

Mr. Granger was out front. He said, "Where we at, Reverend? You convince 'em yet, or are we gonna have to take this up ourselves?"

I could see the man he was talking to held a Bible. He shook his head. Was he really a preacher? Were there two preachers out here doing the Lord's work?

Mr. Granger spoke to Dr. Dobbs. "We meet again, boy. I suggest if you want your family to be alive, you move on out of here tonight. We already warned you."

The lanterns and torches almost made it seem like day outside. I could see Dr. Dobbs's face now. He looked like he was relaxed, standing up straight and tall. I could also see Mr. Granger didn't scare him.

Dr. Dobbs's wife had long hair, and she was very

nice looking. I hadn't really ever looked at the colored people's faces close before. Their skin was so different, but not in a bad way.

Mrs. Dobbs didn't look scared either. I could see a stubborn look on their faces. The Third William spotted me. He smiled.

I didn't smile back. I wished I could have, but I looked down at the ground. They might not be scared. But I felt scared for them. Mr. Granger was dangerous.

"Sir," Dr. Dobbs said, "we bought this land, this house. We own it. And we know our rights under the Constitution of the United States of America. We are Americans just like you."

"No, boy. You're wrong there. You are not like us. We know what y'all trying to do. You stole our jobs, now our houses. What next, our wives?"

I don't know how, 'cause I was terrified, but when Mr. Granger said that, I almost laughed. Dr. Dobbs was a medical doctor. How was he taking Mr. Granger's job? To hear Ma tell it, Mr. Granger was as dumb as a doornail. And I seen Mr. Granger's wife. Ain't no chance Dr. Dobbs trade his pretty wife for Mr. Granger's old hag.

"Let's just get this over with," one of the men said. "I gotta get home to my family."

When the man said this, I suddenly saw something whizz by my head.

The Third William went down on one knee. Someone had hit him with a big rock. His mother knelt down. "Are you all right?"

The Third William stood up. "Yes, I'm fine," he said, his face like granite. "That boy threw a rock at me." He pointed to Phillip. He didn't look scared, just strong, taller and ready to bash anyone who bothered 'em in the face.

I could see blood sliding down into the Third William's eye. His ma tried wiping it off with the bottom of her sweater, but the Third William eased her arm away. "I'm fine."

None of the three Dobbses had on coats. But they didn't seem to be cold.

A car pulled up. Some colored men walked into the yard. Two of them held baseball bats.

One of the taller men said, "Hey, Dobbs. Thought we'd join you for some ball tonight."

These men were huge. One of them had on a maroon and white sweater that said MOREHOUSE COLLEGE.

Mr. Granger said, "I think this is a party you boys weren't invited to."

The man with the sweater slapped the bat into his hand. "Oh, yes we were."

I was waiting for him to hold up his hand the way Miss Fowler did so they could see what I could see—he meant business.

Suddenly I was shaking all over. It was so bad my teeth were chattering together. This was the scaredest I'd ever been in my life.

I looked into Pa's face. I could see it now. Pa didn't want to be standing out here any more than I did.

Out of the corner of my eye I saw Phillip's arm come up. We were close to Mr. Granger, only a few steps back.

I wasn't even thinking when I grabbed Phillip's hand and struggled the rock from him. Me and him went down scuffling together.

Pa pulled me off Phillip. He held us apart. "Stop it. Let's go, son."

Mr. Granger turned around. "What's going on?"

The other men turned too.

"Me and my boy—we're going," Pa said.

Mr. Granger pointed a finger into Pa's chest. "So, you're all a bunch of Negra lovers, hey."

Out of the corner of my eye I could see the colored men forcing Dr. Dobbs and his family into the house.

Mr. Granger turned around and shouted at them, "We'll be back. If you know what's good for you, you'll get out of our side of Reynoldstown. Now, let's go, men. You two walk," he said to me and Pa.

Pa said, "We weren't gonna ride with the likes of you, Granger."

I coughed.

Pa said, "Are you all right, son?"

"Yes, sir," I said. "I'm all right."

We walked side by side. I thought about Dr. Dobbs. I wondered what the white men feared so much about him. 'Cause in my mind my pa and Dr. Dobbs were the real men.

When we got home, Pa didn't say much, he just got his guitar and went in his room.

Ma cleaned my head up where I had opened up my scar, while I told her what happened.

I climbed into bed. Ma come in and said for me to pray for Mr. Granger and the other hating men, 'cause they sure was the ones who needed the Lord.

She didn't even ask me where all the places was Joseph had been. She just rubbed her hand over my hair and said, "You're a good boy."

My muscles ached from the scuffle. I couldn't believe I'd jumped on Phillip. I wanted this to be the end of it, but I knew that couldn't be true. I wondered what Phillip would do if he knew the Third William had been the one to rescue me. I wondered what I would do if he found out too. And there was no chance now he'd let me recite the Freedom Pledge. Ain't that many trades in the world.

★ ONE OF THOSE FOLK ★

Monday morning Ma got let go from her cotton mill job and sent back home. Pa told her he was sorry. And I believe he was.

I was still worried that he was mad at me for getting him in trouble with Mr. Granger and the other men. 'Specially the men from the railroad.

Pa wasn't talking much. That meant he was thinking 'bout things. When him and Joseph would go at it 'bout something, sometimes Pa would go a week not talking to none of us. Then he'd sit down and talk to Joseph, and things would get all right. I was hoping that's what would happen between me and him. But I wasn't gonna bet on it.

I was lonely. If it hadn't been for the Second

Chester, I don't think I coulda made it till the first of January. I still hadn't told my folks that I wasn't gonna be the one reciting the Freedom Pledge. And the teacher didn't know I wanted to do it now. I read over it every chance I got. And every time I got ready to do it, my throat just closed up.

On December 31, Ronnie come back home. I told him about all what had happened.

"I heard of them Columbians. They's really like the Ku Klux Klan. Ma says they evil as water moccasins."

Water moccasins was the feared snakes around our parts. If you went fishing, you worried about water moccasins 'cause they would sneak up on you. Sorta like the Columbians, I guess. Moccasins and Grangers give *herpetons*, what Mr. Little said is Greek for creepy, crawly things that move around on their bellies—a bad name.

Word done got out all over the mill valley that I jumped on Phillip Granger, and it didn't seem like nobody was the sadder for it.

When I got over to Ronnie's house, his ma said I done the right thing. Then she told us she read in the newspaper where two little Negro girls were the first persons to board the Freedom Train in Montgomery,

Alabama. She said people like the Grangers were scared all the poor people would finally come to their senses and gang up on the rich folk instead of each other. She even give me a token out of the Capitula flour for me and Ronnie to go to the Fairview Theatre to see a movie. We wouldn't have to pay the five cents if we had the token.

It was a Roy Rogers movie, *Bells of San Angelo*. It was all right, but it didn't have enough shooting and riding for me. At the end of the movie they showed a short picture of what was coming soon. Me and Ronnie both grinned when we seen it was the special Freedom Train movie that was showing in theaters all across the country. Just to think that my very own brother was on that train every day made me want to stand up taller. On the way home me and Ronnie talked about how much trading stuff we would have once Joseph got home. Joseph done told how he's saving all kinds of souvenirs for me. And Ronnie knows I'll share.

Two other things happened to me that day. For the first time I paid attention that the coloreds had to sit up in the pigeon section, that was the upstairs balcony. And I listened to what they was saying on the screen about the Freedom Train documents. I don't reckon before I thought much about anything except Joseph and the train itself.

That night before I went to bed, I read the poem Joseph had sent me called "Freedom Train," by the Negro poet Langston Hughes. When I got to the part that said,

> If my children ask me, Daddy, please explain
> Why a Jim Crow stations for the Freedom Train?
> What shall I tell my children?
> You tell me, cause freedom ain't freedom when a man ain't free.

I was thinking, *What if Dr. Dobbs gotta tell the Third William that he ain't really free?* And when I thought it, things just come into place, like Joseph said, how you can be seeing something that's wrong, but not really seeing it. I stood up after I read that poem and recited the Freedom Pledge out loud to myself.

I understood it now. And I could understand better,

not all the way, what Joyce was trying to say to me that day. I was one of those folk. Most everyone that I knew, other than the Brookshires and maybe Joseph, was one of those folk. Just like Joyce said, people who don't want to speak up when something ain't right. But for the first time I didn't want to be one of them.

The next morning Ma and Pa was all dressed and ready to go before I even got out of bed. They were so excited about seeing Joseph and the Freedom Train. And to be honest, so was I.

There was only one little problem. I needed to tell them that I wasn't gonna be up there doing the pledge. I was 'bout to tell them when Pa called me into his and Ma's bedroom.

Pa ain't never called me in there before. Him and Joseph had their talks in there, but I ain't never had what Pa called a "man-to-man talk."

I sat down on the soft, cushioned chair Pa fixed special for Ma when I was born. It was kinda worn by now, but real comfortable.

"Son, I been thinking 'bout what happened the other night. Figuring what to tell you 'bout it. And I finally come to the part that I needs to tell you that sometimes men ain't always doing the right thing.

And sometimes other men might go along 'cause they gotta feed their family. You know I ain't no churchgoing Christian, but son, I believe in God and doing right. What I means to say is, you was more of a man than I was the other night. I shouldn'ta gone out there. I know Granger, and to be honest, he ain't no good man. I come up in a different time. We done things to get by. But I don't never want you to follow a man that you know ain't right, son. Your brother done taught me that much."

Pa stood up. "I'm proud of you, Clyde."

And then he tousled my hair.

I couldn't even breathe. Pa never touched my hair or did any kind of mushy stuff. But I knew that this kind of man-to-man talk was what being a man was all about.

And I made up my mind. I was gonna say that Freedom Pledge even if I had to do it while we was standing in the line. Now I understood. My pa might be one, but he didn't want me and Joseph to be one of them folk who just stand by and close up to wrong and, even when they see it outright, don't say a word. No, I would no longer be one of those folk.

★ THE FREEDOM PLEDGE ★

We got on the streetcar together heading for the Freedom Train parked down at the Union Station. I hadn't never seen it so crowded. People was packed in touching. When we got off the streetcar, it was so cold that the freezing rain felt like pins sticking in your skin. Ronnie swears that's when frogs can drop down from the sky. I don't know if it's true or not. I do know I ain't never seen it. But I found myself looking up anyway.

The Freedom Train was staying two days instead of one on account of Birmingham refusing to have the coloreds and whites in the same line.

The line for the train was already long, snaked around from track 6, through the Union Station, up to Spring Street Viaduct and along Marietta Street, down to Marietta and Fairlie. Pa pushed us through the crowds down toward the platform.

We could see another line of folk going to see the train Georgia had on the tracks with some of its famous documents.

The big platform had American flags all over it, and a put-together cover was on top so folk wouldn't get wet.

Miss Fowler was standing on the side at the bottom of the steps to the platform. My folks walked over where she was. I followed, feeling like a man going to be hanged.

Ma said, "Miss Fowler, we done brought the man of the hour with us."

I waited for Miss Fowler to ask her what she was talking about. To tell my parents that Phillip Granger volunteered to recite the Freedom Pledge when their stuttering son chickened out. But instead she just nodded and said, "Great. Now, Clyde, stand right there, don't move until I get back."

I stared after her, my mouth hanging open. What was she on about?

I watched her rush over to the group of students

standing on the platform, dressed like the documents. This was as excited as I'd ever seen her. She was talking real loud. I heard her telling the students to double up.

"You be the Magna Carta. And you be the letter from Robert E. Lee written at the end of the Civil War, as well as your assigned documents."

Then she rushed back over to us. "I need to speak to our man of the hour alone," she said, grabbing me by the arm. "Come on, Clyde, walk over here with me."

Miss Fowler pulled me along, with me looking back every few steps to see if Ma and Pa were still there. Was I dreaming? Maybe that's why Pa tousled my hair like Joseph and Ma usually did. I was still asleep.

Miss Fowler snap-snap-snapped her fingers close to my eyes. "Clyde, quit that daydreaming. And please tell me you still remember the Freedom Pledge."

I thought, *If this is a dream, it won't matter if I say I don't remember.* I laughed, 'cause you can do that kind of thing in a dream, and said, "What Freedom Pledge?"

Miss Fowler looked like she was gonna pass right

out. Then a man in a police uniform come up and said, "The mayor's on his way to the platform. Y'all need to clear the area."

Miss Fowler pinched me—hard. "Clyde Thomason, you better be playing. Come on," she said, leading me away from the platform.

"I'm not dreaming?" I asked her.

"What? Heavens, Clyde, I need you to stop fooling around, because otherwise I need to go find a copy of the pledge and see if you can't quickly brush up on it."

"I'm *not* dreaming? Where's Phillip?"

Miss Fowler sighed. "Do I have to tell you *right now*?"

"Please," I said.

"Oh all right, but quickly. Mr. Little somehow found out what you did at the Negro family's house, and he also found out what Phillip Granger and his father did. Mr. Little called all of us teachers and told us in no uncertain terms that if anybody was going to say the pledge and get the money, it had to be you. To be honest, once I heard what happened, I agreed. Now, are you ready, or are you going to mess up your shoes?"

I said, "No, ma'am, I'm not going to mess up my

shoes. I'm ready. And yes, I do know the Freedom Pledge by heart." I didn't tell her I'd been practicing to say it and that I had made up my mind to say it even if I didn't get on stage.

I ain't gonna lie, I was feeling scared, butterflies was in my stomach and I did feel like I was gonna throw up.

Then I heard Ma squealing. I looked over at her and Pa. Joseph was lifting Ma into the air. He looked so good in his dress blues. His shoes were so shiny, even from here I knew if I got close, I could see my face in them. And there stood Pa in his shiny shoes, and Ma in her new ones.

I forgot about Miss Fowler and ran toward him.

I heard Miss Fowler calling to me, "Listen for your cue to come on stage, now, Clyde Thomason."

Joseph put Ma down when I got up close. "Little brother," he said, hugging me. Only he and Ma hugged me—and boy, had I missed his hugs. He messed my hair. "You ready to recite the pledge?"

Before I could answer, three other guards and a Negro man walked up. The tallest guard said, "So, this must be the young man who is reciting the Freedom Pledge that Joseph's been bragging about."

Joseph said, "Yep, my little brother, Clyde. Oh, Ma, Pa, this is our boss, Lt. Col. Robert F. Scott, and this is Sgt. John Brown, Sgt. Henry "Hank" Steadman, and this is my friend and our porter W. C. Lounds."

I shook the men's hands. I remembered Joseph told me that Colonel Scott, the tall man, was a war hero too.

"Come on, we'll take you on the train," the colonel said. Me, Ma, and Pa followed them onto the train. One part of me hoped I wouldn't miss my turn to speak. The other part of me wished I would.

Once we were on the train, Colonel Scott presented Pa and Ma with a booklet.

I read, "'*The Documents on the Freedom Train*, the American Heritage Foundation,'" like I was reading out loud to myself, so Ma and Pa would know what it was he'd give 'em. They both smiled and told him, "Thank you very much."

We started walking through the train looking at the documents. I would say everything out loud. All of it was going fine until I come to the Bill of Rights. I felt like I should read them carefully on account of Joyce. I could feel my eyes filling up as I read 'em, but

I wasn't gonna cry 'cause Pa was standing right beside me. Then we come to the Constitution. I looked over at Pa and saw a tear comin' down his face.

I couldn't help it. I don't say I know what happened, but I let loose with my tears. Ma was crying already. And then something miracle-like happened. Pa put his arm around me and hugged me.

I couldn't get hold of myself to stop crying. Then Joseph come over and hugged me too. Then Ma.

About that time the colonel said, "Sir, it's time for you to do your duty."

I thought he was talking to Joseph, so I let go of him.

The colonel touched my shoulder, "I'm talking to you, son. The program is starting."

Miss Fowler stood in the train's doorway, motioning for me to hurry up.

I walked out with Joseph, with Ma and Pa right behind us.

"Sit over there and wait for my signal for you to come on stage," Miss Fowler said. "Right after you say the pledge, Joseph will walk up on the stage so that he's beside you when Mayor Hartsfield hands you the check."

I sat down. My leg was shaking, but the butterflies

that was in my stomach was gone. Now there was big old birds flying around in it.

Joseph said, "You can do it, slugger. I told you I met Joe Louis on the train, didn't I?

I nodded. "Ye-e-e-s, y-y-you t-t-t-told me." Oh, no. I was stuttering. I wasn't gonna be able to do it.

Miss Fowler leaned over to me and said, "I forgot to tell you, Phillip's father sent me word a few minutes ago he wasn't allowing Phillip to participate, since the Columbians didn't persuade Mayor Hartsfield to do what Savannah did and find a way to separate the Negroes from the whites in the line. I say good." And then she winked at me and smiled. Mean old Miss Fowler actually smiled!

Things had worked out. Somehow I had been saved from the meanness of Phillip Granger yet again. I had to remember to thank Ronnie special for that rabbit's foot. I squeezed it in my pocket. But now the question was, could I do it? Would I be able to stand up in front of all these people in the cold and rain and say the Freedom Pledge?

Then I saw Mr. Little walking with Dr. Dobbs and his family on the other side of the stage. The Third William waved at me. And I knew.

I could do it. If the Dobbs family could fight off a mob and stay in their house, they deserved to have someone to recite the pledge who understood what it truly meant. Somebody who knew that the Freedom Pledge ain't worth the paper it's written on if it ain't real, and if it ain't for everybody in America.

Miss Fowler said, "It's time. Go on. Get up there, Mr. Clyde Thomason, and make us proud."

Joesph squeezed my hand and said, "I know you can do it, little brother."

I walked up there, still shaking. Still scared, but now determined. I focused my eyes on the Third William. I opened my mouth and out it jumped:

"The Freedom Pledge
I am an American. A free American.
Free to speak—without fear,
Free to worship God in my own way,
Free to stand for what I think right,
Free to oppose what I believe wrong,
Free to choose those who govern my country.
This heritage of Freedom I pledge to uphold
For myself and all mankind."

After the pledge everything became a blur. I heard people clapping. Ma and Pa were actually jumping up and down. Joseph hugged me. The mayor presented me with a check almost big as me. When I left for home that day, I had the best feeling I'd ever had inside my body. I knew what it really meant to be an American.

⋆ FREEDOM ⋆

That night when we was all sitting down to dinner, Ma said a different grace than she usually says over supper.

"For a minute," Pa said, joking, "I thought you was gonna ask God to bless every person you ever met. We're hungry."

I couldn't stop looking at Joseph. He seemed all fired up. "You know, when the Freedom Train tour is over, I want to be one of the folk that help America be the dream it's supposed to be . . . not just for a few people, but for everyone," he said.

Pa said, "Your little brother is growing up to be just like you, son." Pa told Joseph about what happened with the Columbians and how I had jumped on Phillip Granger.

Joseph, Ma, and Pa was saying how proud they was of me when I decided it was time for me to tell them everything.

I told them how I met the Third William and Dr. Dobbs. And how I jumped Phillip 'cause I knew it wouldn't be right for me to stand by and let Phillip hit the Third William again, when he, all by himself, without even knowing me, had stood up for me. I told them how the Third William and Dr. Dobbs had got Mr. Little to find a tree frog for my present. And how Mr. Little said he and Dr. Dobbs was close friends.

The minute I'd let it out, I felt like a big old stone had lifted off my body.

Joseph tousled my hair. "I knew you weren't one of those folk."

I looked at Joseph, my eyes bulging almost out of my head. "Have you been talking to Joyce Brookshire?"

"Nope, I haven't seen her. But I do plan to see her sister while I'm home," Joseph said, winking at Ma.

Pa said, "You know those Brookshires, they try to rule their men."

Joseph said, "So?" And he and Ma burst out laughing.

Pa looked funny.

But I missed what was going on.

———————— ✪ ————————

January 2, I woke up early. Joseph was still asleep. I got dressed quiet so I wouldn't wake him up. He had to go on duty in a few hours. They guarded the documents twenty-four hours a day, seven days a week.

I put on my best pants and shirt, and my new bomber jacket. It was still cold outside, so I pulled on my new wool toboggan. I pushed my hands into my pockets as I walked.

I didn't slow down until I was in front of the Dobbses house. I stood there staring at it. If I didn't know they were in there, I couldn't tell they were Negroes.

I walked up on the porch. I could hear someone singing inside. It must have been the Third William's mother. I knocked on the door, even though I spotted a doorbell as soon as I'd knocked.

After a few minutes Mrs. Dobbs said through the door, "Who is it?"

I took a hard swallow and said, "It's Clyde Thomason. I'm a friend of your son."

Mrs. Dobbs opened the door and I walked inside their home.

Mrs. Dobbs called for the Third William.

The Third William rushed down the stairs. He smiled when he saw me. "Hey," he said.

I said, "Hey," fidgeting with my toboggan.

We stood there for a minute, neither of us saying anything.

I said, "Thanks for the frog."

He said, "You're welcome."

Then we were back to standing and staring at the floor.

Finally the Third William said, "Did you get your Flyer for Christmas like you wanted?"

I said, "I got something better."

"Wow. What did you get? I thought you said that was what you wanted most."

I said, "Yeah, it was."

The Third William said, "Don't keep me in suspense. What was it?"

I stuck out my hand.

The Third William looked puzzled for only a second. Then he said, "Oh," and shook my hand. "You got time to play?"

I said, "You bet."

✧ AUTHOR'S HISTORICAL NOTE ✧

The Freedom Train Pledge scroll was signed by 3.5 million people. Bing Crosby and the Andrews Sisters were a Billboard Top 30 hit singing Irving Berlin's song "Here Comes the Freedom Train," but that song wasn't the only one written for the Freedom Train. Dick Maxwell and Tommy Filas wrote the song, "Freedom Is Everybody's Job" for the Heritage Foundation. Twelve major comic strips, including Mickey Mouse, Blondie, Popeye, Henry, and two special edition comics, were released featuring the Freedom Train. And there were at least ten different Paramount newsreels shown at movie theaters during the two-year span of the train's journey. High school eleventh grader Barbara Flaherty from Lincoln High School in San Francisco, California, penned the essay that won the Quiz Kids High School Student's Scholarship Contest.

Interestingly enough, there were also those who were against the Freedom Train. Not only were there rumored plots to steal the documents, but some people in the United States believed that the Heritage Foundation harbored Communist sympathizers. Others believed that the train itself was a form of government propaganda. It is clear that there was great interest in the train as it criss-crossed the United States, because the FBI had over five hundred pages of information regarding the Freedom Train. (I have copies of those documents.)

Other notes of interest: The original documents numbered 126; however, later another document was added.

The Marine detachment on the train began with twenty-eight guards and officers, but during the two-year period a total of fifty Marines did active duty on the Freedom Train.

Thanks to Craig Harmon of the Lincoln Highway National Museum & Archives, you can see photos, read press releases and news articles, hear the Freedom Train theme song, and even listen to radio programs about the Freedom Train on his website at http://www.lincoln-high way-museum.org/FT/FT-Index.html.

Also, the U.S. Marine Corps magazine, *The Leatherneck*, and *National Geographic* have wonderful articles about the Freedom Train. You can also visit the National Archives in College Park, Maryland, to see the original documents.

I did embrace a few historical licenses in this story, and I'll tell you what they are: The Captain Marvel comic book with the Freedom Train on the cover was published in June 1948. I own this comic, by the way. I also own the Archie comic mentioned in the story. The Freedom Train didn't go to San Francisco until March 1948. And the comic strips Lil' Abner and Joe Palooka did feature the Freedom Train, but I ignored their publication dates. And if you consult a calendar for 1947, Christmas fell on a Thursday, not Sunday, like it is in this story.

Clyde Thomason began speaking to me one day as I stared at some newspaper clippings about the 1947–1948 Freedom Train. Until that time I had attempted to tell this story in a young African-American boy's voice. But something just didn't work. Once I met Clyde, I knew it was his story.

I felt grateful to include the historic village of Cabbagetown, in Atlanta. This is a small community that was built up around a cotton mill, like many small neighborhoods in the South during that era. Luckily for me, many of the people (all white) who grew up in Cabbagetown were willing to share their stories, anecdotes, and feelings about their life during that time.

I also thought it was important to tell the story of the poor working class in Georgia, people who weren't treated much better than African Americans during the 1940s and '50s. Often, in the southern towns, like in Atlanta, these people found themselves pitted against African Americans who they believed were taking their jobs. Too many stories portray these people as ignorant bigots, but that had not been my experience, and I wanted to give voice to Clyde Thomason.

I am from the South. And even though I wasn't old enough to visit the Freedom Train, I have a special place in my spirit for the notion of it. And because I feel strongly about immigration, class, and prejudice, I felt I was the right person to write this story. I understand intimately the dynamics of the South and how it forced its citizens through laws and emotional resonance to hate one another. But I also recognize the great significance of those few people, both black and white, who fought to change those laws.

I also found it fascinating that the mayor of Atlanta took a stand against other southern mayors in order to integrate the lines to view the Freedom Train. After reading many of Mayor Hartsfield's personal papers, and reviewing some of his decisions before and after the Freedom Train's visit to Atlanta, I am still puzzled that he allowed the integrated lines. The South and its people, both black and white, traversed dangerous and oftentimes unpredictable waters to get to the shores of integration.

But more importantly, I cared about this story and its impact on children today and tomorrow. And I believe that Clyde Thomason knew my heart when he whispered his tale into my ears.

In Alexandria, Virginia, a twenty-eight-man Marine detachment is inspected before boarding the Freedom Train to begin its tour in September 1947. Marines lived and rode aboard the train, guarding its precious contents and serving as hosts to visitors.

Courtesy of National Archives (photo no. 200-AAF-46-1)

The Freedom Train's porters, handpicked World War II veterans, took care of the onboard quarters and protected the personal property of those who traveled with the train. Above is the crew that accompanied the Freedom Train from New York City to Boston, Massachusetts.

Courtesy of National Archives (photo no. 200-AHF-59-1)

The organizers of the Freedom Train's journey, including President Harry S. Truman and U.S. Attorney General Tom Clark, ordered that viewing of the exhibit not be segregated. Consequently, the train did not stop in several towns whose mayors refused to abide by this guideline. The Freedom Train did, however, stop in Pine Bluff, Arkansas, whose non-segregated crowd waited in line on January 21, 1948 (shown above).

Deet's world turns upside down when his father is sent to prison.

"Compelling." —*Booklist*

"A sensitive, courageous protagonist who is smart enough
and open-minded enough to look past people's mistakes."
—*Publishers Weekly*

The fire was only the beginning. . . .

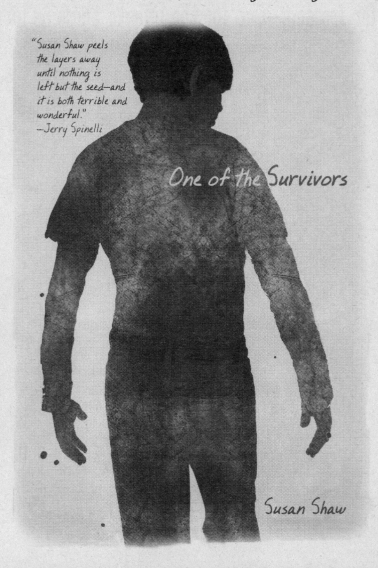

"Susan Shaw peels the layers away until nothing is left but the seed—and it is both terrible and wonderful."
—Jerry Spinelli

One of the Survivors

Susan Shaw

EBOOK EDITION ALSO AVAILABLE

From Margaret K. McElderry Books | Published by Simon & Schuster | TEEN.SimonandSchuster.com

A thrilling adventure of a boy galloping furiously for freedom—and for the lives of those he loves.

"Appealing, energetic, and provocative."
—*School Library Journal*

"An exciting and entertaining read."
—Zilpha Keatley Snyder, three—time Newbery
Honor—winning author of *The Egypt Game*

Booklist Editors' Choice

NYPL Book for the Teen Age

Spur Award Winner (Western Writers of America)

VOYA Top Shelf Fiction for Middle School Readers

Published by Margaret K. McElderry Books * Simon & Schuster Children's Publishing
KIDS.SimonandSchuster.com